Vineyard Prey

Vineyard Prey

A Martha's Vineyard Mystery

Philip R. Craig

THORNDIKE

CHIVERS

This Large Print edition is published by Thorndike Press®, Waterville, Maine USA and by BBC Audiobooks, Ltd, Bath, England.

Published in 2005 in the U.S. by arrangement with Scribner, an imprint of Simon & Schuster Inc.

Published in 2005 in the U.K. by arrangement with the author.

U.S. Hardcover 0-7862-7614-2 (Mystery)
U.K. Hardcover 1-4056-3489-8 (Chivers Large Print)

The text of this Large Print edition is unabridged. Other aspects of the book may vary from the original edition.

Set in 16 pt. Plantin by Liana M. Walker.

Printed in the United States on permanent paper.

British Library Cataloguing-in-Publication Data available

Library of Congress Cataloging-in-Publication Data

Craig, Philip R., 1933–
    Vineyard prey : a Martha's Vineyard mystery /
    by Philip R. Craig.
        p. cm. — (Thorndike Press large print mystery)
    ISBN 0-7862-7614-2 (lg. print : hc : alk. paper)
    1. Jackson, Jeff (Fictitious character) — Fiction.
2. Private investigators — Massachusetts — Martha's
Vineyard — Fiction. 3. Martha's Vineyard (Mass.) —
Fiction. 4. Large type books.   I. Title.
II. Thorndike Press large print mystery series.
PS3553.R23V529 2005b
    813'.54—dc22   2005007288

For the founders and friends
of the Seventh Street Yacht Club:

Neil and Elaine Patt,
Charlie and Eva Carlson,
Mike and Cathy Smith,
Bill and Linda Searle,
Olga Church,
Bill and Kathy Morgan,
Bob Erlandson,
Jim and Elsie Connell,
Arvin and Jean Wells,
and Tim and Ruth Cogen.

O rose, thou art sick:
The invisible worm
That flies in the night,
In the howling storm,

Has found out thy bed
Of crimson joy,
And his dark secret love
Does thy life destroy.

— William Blake
The Sick Rose

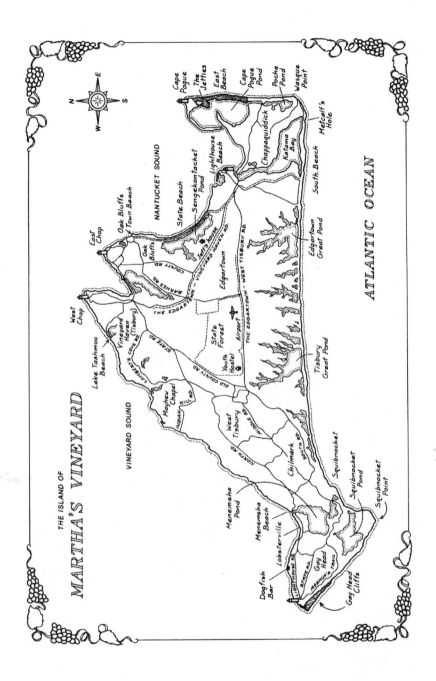

THE ISLAND OF
MARTHA'S VINEYARD

1

There was a time when the tourist season on Martha's Vineyard pretty much began on the Fourth of July and ended on Labor Day. Increasingly, however, the shoulder seasons have expanded. People start coming down for weekends in April or even earlier, and the island doesn't really belong to islanders again until after New Year's, when, for two months, it's ours alone, and is very quiet.

Of the Vineyard's two shoulder seasons, the fall and winter shoulder is the busiest, what with childless couples staying to enjoy the autumn weather and off-island people returning for the annual Bass and Bluefish Derby, deer-hunting season, weddings, Columbus Day, Thanksgiving, and Christmas.

January and February, the quiet months, are perplexities to off-islanders, who often ask, "What do you *do* down there during the winter?" and proclaim that being penned up on an island would drive them crazy from boredom. For Vineyarders, on the other hand, being penned up on the mainland would be much worse.

The difference between the two groups is that the off-islanders need to be able to travel about on the spur of the moment, whereas Vineyarders accept the fact that they must live by ferry schedules and reservation policies. If your psychic welfare depends upon instant mobility — going to the mall, the opera, the Kittery Trading Post, or wherever — you shouldn't live on an island.

Off-islanders also err in thinking that there's nothing to do on the Vineyard during the winter. In fact, there's so much to do that you can't begin to do it all. There are community chorus rehearsals and performances and other musical activities and presentations; there are reading groups, amateur theatrics, movies, learned lectures, and high school sporting events; you can ice fish or go frostbite sailing, hunting, ice boating, dancing, or partying. If you want to, you can be out every night, sopping up culture or just having a good time. If you're bored, it's probably because you are a bore.

Zee and I and the two kids attend some of these many events but in general prefer to stay at home with each other in our old but cozy onetime hunting-camp home. Nothing pleases me more than being inside with my family, warm in front of the glass-doored living room stove while the winter wind howls outside and snow splats against the windows.

We have all the entertainment we need right here: shelves of books, a good radio, the last black-and-white TV in the world, a stereo system for our tapes and CDs, and our recently purchased computer, which is mostly used by Joshua and Diana for their schoolwork and which has temporarily put a stop to their previously consistent pleas for a dog.

I know that when the new wears off the computer, the dog request will return with more of "But all our friends have dogs, Pa," and "We'd take care of it ourselves, Pa," and all the other pleas and promises. But I am not about to have a dog. No dogs! We have cats: Oliver Underfoot and Velcro.

Cats are quiet and independent, but dogs are yappy and born slaves who want nothing more than to serve their masters.

In fact, of course, their owners are the real slaves, constantly walking, feeding, and cleaning up after their noisy, slobbering pets. I don't approve of slaves or slavery, so we're not going to have a dog if I have anything to say about it! Whenever I preach this sermon, Zee rolls her great dark eyes and shakes her beautiful head.

The trouble began in early December, during deer season, when the kids were still under the spell of the computer and we were all beginning to think Christmas thoughts.

In our house, we don't consider it proper to do anything Christmasy until after Thanksgiving, and we feel free to raise disapproving eyebrows when stores offer pre-Thanksgiving Christmas music or displays or sales of Christmas items.

"Do you think we're getting stuffier about this Christmas thing as we get older?" asked Zee, as we strolled Edgartown's Main Street.

"Absolutely not," I said. "It's like the Good Book says: for everything there is a season."

"This isn't a case of the devil quoting scripture, is it?"

"No comment."

"Do you approve of having deer-hunting season between Thanksgiving and Christmas? Does the Good Book have anything to say about that?"

I took her arm in mine. "You're just trying to start trouble."

"Who, me?"

There are a lot of deer on Martha's Vineyard and every year hunters kill several hundred of them. There's a season for shotguns, one for muzzle-loaders, and one for bows and arrows. Other deer are shot out of season by hunters who don't wait for state approval to ply their ancient art.

About the same number of deer are killed each year by cars, which raises the question of what sort of license you really need to bag your buck.

The island's most passionate opponents of hunters and hunting are members of VETA, Vineyarders for the Ethical Treatment of Animals, which is the local version of a national organization, or perhaps it's an international organization, devoted to nonviolence to all creatures.

My friend Mimi Bettencourt Cortez belongs to VETA, although her views did not prevent her from marrying Ignacio "Nash" Cortez, who is as dedicated a hunter and fisherman as Mimi is a dedicated vegetarian. Mimi also has a sense of humor, which seems nonexistent in many of her VETA comrades.

Nash, in response to his wife's support of VETA, has created his own organization, VETFAV, Vineyarders for the Ethical Treatment of Fruits and Vegetables, which is dedicated to decrying the heartless killing, mutilation, torture, and devouring of innocent plants. Nash's letters to the papers have gotten a lot of laughs from hunters and fishermen and even a few from Mimi, but the rest of the VETA people are not amused.

I eat a lot of plants and I'm also a fan of venison cooked rare. I used to shoot my own deer, but somehow the joy of the hunt faded for me, and I put my shotguns away with the rifle my father used when he hunted in Maine. I disapprove of trophy hunters but I have no moral objections whatever about hunting and fishing as long as the hunters and fishermen eat what they kill. If you eat it you can kill it, as far as I'm concerned, although I admit to drawing the line at killing and eating people.

I can't really think of a strictly logical reason for making that exception, but I do make it, probably because of some irrational bias favoring my species; I've wondered if we'd have fewer or more wars if soldiers were required to eat the enemies they killed.

Without getting too involved in the moral subtleties of killing things, I'll add here that I think it's also okay to kill something or someone who's trying to kill or seriously damage you or yours. Finally, to complicate my ethics a bit more, I should say that although I disapprove of capital punishment (because mistakes often have and will continue to be made in trials), I think there are some people who deserve to be killed and whose deaths would greatly improve society.

I generally favor leaving them to the police and the courts, but a guy I know, having given thought to the matter over a few beers, came to a different conclusion. He was of the opinion that capital punishment should be outlawed but duels should be allowed. The participating parties would need to be in agreement about the terms and the matter would be personal instead of abstract, two factors that seemed to my acquaintance to legitimize the affair in some way. When I asked him about motives for shooting or stabbing other people under the great oak at dawn, he thought the classic ones would do: revenge for insults and hurts, real or imagined.

Most killers, however, are not so fearless and foolishly honorable as to stand in front of their equally armed adversaries and stab or fire on command. They prefer assassination. One such person came to the Vineyard when the island hunters were shooting deer and I was doing some scalloping over in Cape Pogue Pond, sharing Mike Look's boat and paying for my share of expenses to drag my limit along with his. The killer was after bigger game.

I got involved while I was opening my day's catch of scallops out in the shed behind our house, glad to be out of the wind and near the kerosene heater that took the chill from the afternoon air. I worked wearing a rubberized apron and standing at a table holding scallops I'd dumped there from my bushel baskets. I had a fifty-gallon barrel for the emptied shells, a stainless steel bowl for the meat I cut, and a smaller bowl of water in case I needed to rinse something. My scalloping knife was an old, familiar one, and with it I could work my way through a bushel in pretty good time. I'm not the fastest opener I know, but I'm not the slowest, either. When you get paid by the pound, you have to be fast and steady and you don't want to leave any meat on the shells.

When I filled the stainless steel bowl, I'd take it to the house and get another one. Zee would pack the scallops in plastic containers to sell to the local markets. Fresh bay scallops are hard to beat for taste and usually bring a price that makes dragging for them and opening them worthwhile. There is irony involved, of course: the more scallops there are, the more quickly you can get your limit, but the lower the price. And vice versa. There ain't no justice in this world, as the old-timers say. The market owners naturally disagree.

I was working on my last quarter bushel of scallops when the shed door opened behind me. I glanced back and saw Joe Begay. He had a hand in the pocket of his winter camouflage jacket, and he scanned the woods behind the shed before shutting the door.

Joe and I went back all the way to America's last Asian war, when he had been my sergeant and I had been a seventeen-year-old who had lied about his age to become a soldier. My military career had been a short one: on my very first patrol Joe and I had both gotten blown up by a Viet Cong

17

mortarman who had sighted us before we sighted him.

The mortarman had done his work well and Joe and I spent a lot of time in hospitals. My legacy was considerable scar tissue and shrapnel below my knees. Joe Begay's was eye damage that had blinded him for a time and still obliged him to wear dark glasses under most conditions. But we had both been luckier than others on that patrol.

I occasionally still have dreams about the incredible noise of the attack, and about the flying dirt and brush and body parts, and I will wake making sounds for which there are no names as Zee, who is a nurse who knows how to take care of both my body and soul, gently shakes me and tells me everything is all right, that she is there and we are far from war.

Now, years after that fatal ambush, Joe and I both lived on Martha's Vineyard, albeit on opposite ends of the island. Joe, who had married Toni Vanderbeck, of the Aquinnah Vanderbecks, was supposedly retired after decades of government work he didn't discuss but that still occasionally took him away from home for days or even weeks at a time. Where he went or what he did I never asked, which was perhaps why we had remained friends.

"You could get yourself shot wearing a jacket like that during deer season," I said, going back to work. "How are you at opening scallops?"

"Out in Oraibi we didn't have scallops," said Begay.

That was true. There were no scallops on Third Mesa or anywhere else on the Hopi reservation. Begay was a long way from his boyhood Arizona home.

"Well, now that you're married to a Wampanoag and live in Wampanoagland and have kids who are half Wampanoag, you should make an effort to master Wampanoag skills. The Wampanoags have been opening Vineyard scallops for ten thousand years."

"I'm not sure about the ten thousand years, but otherwise you're probably right," said Begay.

Something in his tone caused me to turn and look at him again. He was bent and looking through the small, dirty window in the back wall toward the woods that lead off from our buildings toward the Felix Neck wildlife sanctuary.

He was a tall man, big through the shoulders and chest but lean from the waist down. His hair was shiny, straight,

19

and black as the Pit. His face was brown, his eyes were black, and his cheekbones were high. His wife, Toni, when describing their first meeting out in Santa Fe, said she had never seen anybody who looked more like an Indian was supposed to look and that she had fallen instantly in love with him.

"What's out there?" I asked him. "Some deer hunter? I don't post my land and I don't mind them hunting, but I'd like them to do it farther from the house."

"I don't see anything at all," said Begay, straightening. "I was just double-checking my trail. I parked over at Felix Neck."

Interesting. "You came through the woods? Why don't you use the driveway like everybody else?"

"Next time."

The air seemed to change, to become thinner, more brittle. I turned back to the table, but my hands were acting on their own as they worked through the remaining scallops. "What's going on?" I asked.

"I need a favor."

"Ask."

"I'm driving to Hyannis tomorrow morning. I'd like to have you pick me up there and bring me back to the island."

"All right."

"I'll explain later."

"All right."

"It's probably best not to tell Zee any more than you have to. There may be strangers around asking questions, and she can't tell them what she doesn't know."

"I trust her as much as I trust myself."

"Use your own judgment, then. Drive to the Cape Cod Mall about noon and get yourself some lunch in the food court. I'll meet you there."

"All right. Are Toni and the kids okay?"

"I've sent them away. I'll tell you about it tomorrow."

"Do you need anything? A place to stay tonight? Something to eat or drink?" I paused, then added, "A weapon?"

"No. Thanks. I'll see you tomorrow."

"Yes." I turned when I heard the door unlatch. He still had his hand in the side pocket of his jacket. He studied the woods and left, shutting the door behind him. I went to the window and watched him move away, walking swiftly and gracefully. The winter camouflage blended well with the barren December forest and he was soon out of sight. I studied the woods awhile longer but saw no other movement.

I finished opening the scallops and carried the meat into the house.

"This is the last of them," I said to Zee. "I'll dump the shells."

I went out and put the barrel into the back of my rusty old Toyota Land Cruiser and took it up to the spot off Clevelandtown Road where scallopers dump their shells. A small flock of seagulls was there before me, picking at shells and making resentful noises as they flew up and waited for me to go away and leave them to their feast.

I dumped my barrel and drove on up to the airport, where I got round-trip ferry reservations for the next day. In December that's easier than in the summer, when it's virtually impossible because of the tourists.

At home, our outdoor pipes had been drained for the winter, so I used a bucket of water from the kitchen to rinse out the barrel before leaving it upside down to drain beside the shed.

Then I returned to the house. Already the sun was low in the western sky, and Joshua and Diana would soon be home from the second grade and kindergarten. I wanted to talk with Zee before they arrived.

Zee had the last of the scallops in the fridge and was working on supper. Scallops, of course. Her plan, I saw, was to fry them up with garlic butter and serve them over rice with broccoli on the side. A winning meal, for sure.

I washed up and prepared the broc for the microwave. We were becoming very twenty-first-century-ish, what with our microwave, our cell phone, and our computer. The next thing you know we'll be getting a color TV.

While I worked, Zee told me we'd gotten a call from Professor Buford Oakland, who wanted me to open up his Oak Bluffs house for family members who would be making a pre-Christmas trip to the island. I added his house to the list of several others I also had to open for the holidays, and told her about Joe Begay's visit to the shed.

She frowned. "He said that he sent Toni and the children away? I called her yesterday and got her answering machine. I was wondering why she never called back. What do you suppose is going on?"

"I'll tell you when I know."

"I don't like it so far. I wonder where Toni is."

"I don't like it either," I said, "but maybe there's nothing to worry about."

"Where are Joshua and Diana?" asked

Zee, glancing at the wall clock. "They should be home by now."

"The bus doesn't get them here for another ten or fifteen minutes," I said in my soothing voice.

"Are you sure Joe had a pistol in his pocket?"

"It looked that way to me."

"I don't like it. Should we call the police?"

"If Joe wanted the police I think he'd have called them."

The cats, Oliver Underfoot and Velcro, came into the room and suggested that it was time for their afternoon snack. I gave it to them. A quarter of an hour later Joshua and Diana strolled down our long sandy driveway right on schedule.

Everything at the Jackson house seemed normal, but to Zee and me everything had changed.

2

I took our mainland shopping list with me when I went over to Cape Cod the next morning, because normal life doesn't stop in abnormal times and when you live on Martha's Vineyard, you never come home from America with an empty car. You fill it full of stuff that you can buy for a fraction of what it would cost on the island, and you always fill your tank with mainland gasoline before catching the ferry home.

Since most Cape Cod stores are open at nine and it can take an hour to drive from the Woods Hole ferry terminal to Hyannis, I'd reserved an early-morning trip from Vineyard Haven so I'd have a couple of hours to shop before meeting Joe Begay at the mall at noon. I drove Zee's little Jeep since it was less conspicuous than my antique Land Cruiser.

On the way to the ferry, though, I

stopped at two of the houses I look after during the winter. Since I have no regular job, I stretch out my meager disability money by fishing, doing odd jobs, and caretaking several houses. I close them in the fall, check on them during the winter, and open them again in the spring or whenever their owners want them opened.

In this case, both of my stops were to open houses for Christmas. This included turning up the thermostats and making sure that all windows and doors were locked and that there were no signs of illegal entry or other problems. In the Oakland house I lingered awhile in the library, which was a room I loved.

Professor Buford Oakland was a friend of my friend Professor John Skye, who had recommended me for the job with the Oaklands. John was a medieval lit man at Weststock College, up north of Boston, and Oakland was a historian with a focus on the Civil War. He taught somewhere in Virginia and was, I guessed by his name, a Southerner himself, since no one but a Southerner would be named Buford. He was a Yale man, which perhaps explained how he ended up with a summer place on the Vineyard, although a surprising number of Southerners have island houses.

Buford Oakland had a couple of grown children I'd never met, and like John Skye, he had a large library that I admired; but whereas the only weaponry on display in John's library was a triangulation of foil, épée, and saber on a wall, a token of John's athletic career as a collegiate three-weapon man, Oakland had a private collection of Civil War memorabilia including bayonets, pistols, and rifles on a wall and in a glass-covered case below it. Among these was a LeMat revolver that sported a short shotgun barrel below the cylinder, in case you missed nine times with the regular bullets, and a Type II 1863 rifle-musket made by the Springfield Armory that was, according to the little card beside it, the last regulation U.S. muzzle-loader. Firearms had changed quite a bit since the Blue and the Gray went at it, and I marveled, as always, at the amount of human ingenuity that went into developing ways of killing and maiming other humans.

Dr. Oakland also had battlefield maps and shelves of books about the war, including some he had written himself. It was clear that he loved his subject, and I guessed that that love probably made him an exciting teacher. One of the Vineyard's charms is that it has more than its share of interesting residents, and you never know when you're going to encounter one of them. Before leaving the room, I laid paper, kindling, and wood in the fireplace. Whoever was coming might enjoy a good book in front of a fire on a cold December night.

Hearing a lone shot off in the woods to my right as I left the house, I remembered my father once telling me that if you heard a single shot, the chances were good that the hunter got his deer; that if you heard two shots the chances were not so good; and that if you heard three shots the deer was still running. In muzzle-loader days, you only got one chance, which was part of the charm for modern-day black-powder hunters, who liked the link to their ancestral shooters. The thrill of the hunt must be buried deep in our genetic codes.

After I drove off the ferry in Woods Hole, I hit most of the stores in Falmouth where Vineyarders traditionally shop: Kappy's for booze, the Christmas Tree Shop and the Oceanstate Job Lot for dolmas and serendipitous discoveries, Wal-Mart for birdseed, toilet paper, paper towels, and a few other items on Zee's list, and the office-supply place for computer paper and ink. I also got a late breakfast at

McDonald's because there are no McDonald's on Martha's Vineyard and I always
pig out at Mac's when I go off-island.

At the Cape Cod Mall in Hyannis I had
another McDonald's meal for lunch in the
food court: a double cheeseburger, tall
fries, and a medium Coke. Two Mac meals
in a single day. Heaven.

Joe Begay didn't join me. Instead, as he
walked by my table he said, sotto voce,
"Drive by the door at the far end of the
mall in half an hour. I'll be there." He
walked on and I kept eating. When I was
through, I went out to the Jeep and drove
to the other end of the mall. As I eased
past the entrance there, Joe Begay appeared. I stopped and he slid into the seat
beside me.

"Drive," he said, looking back toward
the entrance.

I did that, glancing into the rearview
mirror and seeing no one who appeared to
be interested in us.

"Home, James," said Begay, sliding his
big body down as far as it would go, which
was not enough to get his head below the
level of the windows.

I drove out onto Route 28 and headed
for Woods Hole. "When we get down the
road a way," I said, "we'll pull off and fix

you a nest in the backseat. You can hide in the toilet paper."

"Fine." Begay sat back up in the seat. "I feel like somebody in a Hitchcock film."

"Me, too. Where's your truck?"

"At the airport."

The Hyannis airport is almost across the street from the mall.

"That may cause some confusion among the heathen," I said.

"I hope so," said Begay. "When's your reservation back to the island?"

"Middle of the afternoon. You need some time to do something first?"

"No. Just get me back to the Vineyard. When we get there, can you take me up to the house? Toni's car's there."

"Sure."

We drove on.

"You're not asking many questions," said Begay.

"Not because I don't have them. You want to bunk out with us for a while?"

"No need. I may be imagining things but if I'm right, I don't want to get you any more involved."

"I'm already involved. I just don't know in what."

"You're not involved yet. I'm sure nobody trailed me out of the mall, so you're clear if you get me back to the house without anyone seeing me with you."

My rearview mirror was empty. "I can do that," I said, "but you're wrong about me not being involved. I've been involved with you since you saved my bacon in 'Nam."

"I'm the one whose bacon got saved by you," said Begay. "Are we ever going to get this story straight?"

I glanced at him and saw a small smile on his craggy face. "Probably not," I said.

When the Vietnam mortarman had dropped his rounds on us, blinded Sergeant Begay had picked up shrapnel-crippled me and become my legs while I had become his eyes. Two half-men had become one whole man long enough to call in the gunships and the medics and to save what was left of our patrol. The argument about who had saved whom had gone on ever since and had become a joke.

Now, after Begay said nothing for a while, I asked, "Where are Toni and the kids?"

"I sent them out to Arizona to spend some time with my people. I told Toni to take the children out of school for a couple of weeks and show them where their daddy grew up. She didn't want to go, but she

31

went. They should be fine. The Easter Bunny has never been there."

I drove for a while before I said, "The Easter Bunny. It's the wrong time of year for the Easter Bunny. It's almost time for Rudolph."

"It's not Rudolph," said Begay. "We got Rudolph. And we got the Scarecrow, too, but we don't think we got the Easter Bunny."

Most of the souvenir shops along Route 28 were closed for the winter. I saw one such and pulled around behind it. We repacked the backseat with Begay snuggled between a large pack of toilet paper and an even larger pack of paper towels. All he had to do to be invisible was to hold a fifty-pound sack of oiled sunflower seeds in his lap. I found the case of Sam Adams I'd gotten earlier at Kappy's and gave us each one before we started on down the road again.

"If you don't want to tell me what this is about," I said, "I won't push it. I'll ask Jake Spitz."

"I deserve this," said Begay. "I'd forgotten how nosy you can be."

That wasn't true, of course. Joe Begay didn't forget things. He thought he might need someone and that he could trust me if push came to shove. He was right about the trust, but I was more than two decades past soldiering so I hoped he wouldn't need any honed combat skills.

"I'll go to Jake if I have to," I said, "but it might save some time if you came right out with it."

"Jake is FBI," said Begay. "This involves other people."

"If you say so. Okay, let's talk about something else. How about them Patriots? They gonna make it to the Super Bowl this year?"

There was a silence, then Joe said, "All right, here's what I know. In the last few months three people I worked with on a job have been killed. The odds of those three people dying in one year seem pretty long, especially since the last two died Stateside. There are two of us left."

"Overseas work," I said, taking note of the Stateside reference.

"Unofficially, yes; officially, no comment. Last year five of us were on a trade mission abroad to drum up business for some American corporations. We courted officials and businesspeople and tried to open some closed doors. The State Department worked with us because they agree with old Cal that the business of

33

America is business."

"What was your real job?"

"That actually was one of our real jobs, and we managed to make some progress. We were so good that our cover seemed perfect." He paused. "Of course we had another job, and we made progress on that one, too. Ever read about the hashshashin, back in Crusader days?"

"Yes. The killers who did their work high on hash and religion. The original assassins."

"Well, the modern equivalents are still around. Some of them are the suicide bombers you read so much about. Nowadays, though, the top guys are more interested in money than religion, and they never die for the cause if they can get somebody else to do it for them. They hang out in safe countries and usually do their jobs somewhere else.

"The world being what it is, there's plenty of work for them and they do it well, and when they go home afterwards they live in fine houses and are very law-abiding and generous. They build schools and sewer systems and hospitals, and the local people love them at least as much as they fear them."

"Sounds like life in parts of South America."

"There and other places, too. They pay local officials and police to leave them alone and since they have more money than God and do their killing in other countries, most of them die peacefully in bed, surrounded by grieving wives and children. They're hard to find and harder to stop because their security and intelligence systems are so good and because the authorities mostly turn a blind eye on them."

"Crime pays pretty well sometimes."

"But not all the time. The sword of Damocles hangs over every crowned head, and there are always people who lose when the hashshashin win and they get mad and try to get even. Some of those people live in the U.S.A."

I could imagine who some of them might be: bigwigs in the alphabet-soup intelligence and military organizations in Washington who are after the heads of people they perceive as opposed to American interests. The more violent the opposition, the greater the anger and desire for vengeance.

"Terrorists," I said. It was the currently favored term for such enemies, although, of course, one man's terrorist is another man's hero just as one man's traitor is another's patriot. Benedict Arnold, Major André, and Nathan Hale had been three of the latter during the American Revolution. What sort of men they were depended on whom you asked.

"Whatever," said Begay. "What happened was that two of three people who interested us came to bad ends during that particular trade mission. The third one got away."

"The Easter Bunny."

"Yes. The current Washington wisdom is that it's taken the Bunny a while to figure out what happened to his friends and to do something about it. He probably figures we're the terrorists and he's the heroic avenger."

"How'd he get that code name?"

"The three of them specialized in blowing people up during religious holidays. Christmas, Easter, Passover, Ramadan, and so forth. The one we called the Scarecrow had his biggest success on All Hallows' Eve in London, Rudolph set off a bomb in Bethlehem on Christmas morning, and the Easter Bunny did the same in a cathedral in Bosnia on Good Friday. It's a good way to attract people's attention."

"Why is he after your group? I didn't know there was much loyalty among people in that business."

"Revenge is always popular. In any case, the Bunny has done the right thing for himself. He's showed the world that his intelligence is as good as anybody's and that he can kill you no matter where you live. It's good for his business."

I thought about that, then said, "Most accidents happen in the home. He may not live where he used to live, but he must live somewhere."

"We think we know where, but in this case he lives in a country that likes his work and isn't about to let anyone get at him. We have assets inside the borders, of course, and we're spreading money around to get local people on our side, but so far no luck. Meanwhile, the Bunny can come and go as he pleases, provided he avoids the national airports, where he might be spotted by our people."

"And you think he's here in the States right now."

"That's the theory."

As we came into Falmouth, Joe arranged the bag of birdseed in front of him. You have to arrive at the ferry dock a half hour before the boat leaves, so he was going to have to sit there quietly for quite a while if he was to be unobserved.

I got into the parking lot line and turned on the Cape's classical station. It plays fine instrumental music but never any opera arias or choral music because, I was told when I asked why, studies show that audiences of classical music decline significantly when vocal music is offered. Since I consider the human voice to be the finest of musical instruments, I find this inexplicable, and I split my radio time between the classical station and the country-and-western station in Rhode Island. C-and-W fans like human voices, even nasal ones.

"Do you have a plan for the Bunny?" I asked Joe.

"I do," he replied in a muffled voice from beneath the birdseed. "I plan to kill him."

3

There were not many leaves on the trees, so as I drove to Aquinnah I could see farther into the woods than I can in the summer. Narrow, sandy driveways led to houses and barns and stone fences that for half the year were invisible from the road, the property of people who like their privacy.

Today there were many hunters out there somewhere, seeking deer, and maybe one hunter seeking Joe Begay. Joe had removed the bag of birdseed from his lap when we'd passed Lake Tashmoo, and in my rearview mirror I could see him looking thoughtfully out the window.

"What can you tell me about this guy?" I asked. "What does he look like? Where does he come from?"

"Remember Carlos the Jackal?"

Who could forget the world's most wanted hired assassin? I said, "I think he was from South America someplace. He had a very long run, but they finally got him and put him in jail. Are you telling me that the Easter Bunny looks like Carlos?"

"No, because we really aren't too sure what the Bunny looks like. We have some fuzzy photos and some supposedly eyewitness descriptions, but about all we know is that he's not too tall, is on the skinny side, and is probably of European descent. We can't even be sure he's not a woman. The point is that, like Carlos, the Bunny works as an assassin for organizations the U.S.A. doesn't like at all, and has been at it for a long time, very successfully." Begay paused, then added, "Too successfully, in my book."

"European descent?"

"Apparently, according to the eyewitnesses I mentioned. I doubt if they really know, but maybe one of them heard the Bunny talk about his childhood or his school, or something like that. Anyway, the Scarecrow and Rudolph worked mostly, but not always, in the Middle East and Africa, but the Easter Bunny almost always worked north of the Med, probably because he has European looks. The Scarecrow and Rudolph were both darker-skinned."

"And now he's in America? Does he speak English?"

"He speaks a dozen languages, they say."

"Any accent?"

"I don't know. He probably doesn't talk like an American since as far as we know he has never lived in the States."

"Until now."

"Maybe not even now. Maybe he flew in and out to do the two Stateside jobs."

"In spite of Homeland Security?"

Begay smiled a small, grim smile. "In spite of that. The homeland isn't as secure as Washington wishes it was. The Bunny can probably get in and out and move around pretty freely without being noticed."

That was no doubt true. Americans are amazingly free of police surveillance in spite of what civil libertarians currently see as intrusions into private lives by the authorities. Not that a lot of those authorities aren't glad to intrude and will continue to try to do so on the grounds that security is more important than freedom. People like that are scarier to me than are most professional criminals.

"Does he know where you live?" I asked.

"My address here isn't top secret," said Begay. "But before I sent Toni and the kids out to Third Mesa, I talked to some of my family there and they said nobody had been around asking questions. If someone had, he wouldn't have gotten a very clear answer."

I'd read once that the Hopi language was of such a nature that for its speakers, time and space are perceived differently than they are for English speakers; that the language has no words for small segments of time, but only indications that events are not happening anymore, are still happening, or may happen in the future, and that people, too, are no longer here or are here or may be here in the future. It was a good language to hide in with perfect honesty.

"But the Bunny knows you're here on the island."

"I think he could find out," said Begay. "Like I say, it's not a secret. Some people in Washington know. Other people know. And I'm probably listed on some computer site."

"Does the Bunny have access to military records?" I asked.

"Probably, because those records really aren't too secure." Then he surprised me by saying, "That's why I played this little Hyannis airport game. I want him to think

I'm here, but that I tried to fool him into thinking I left. If he's as smart as he's supposed to be, he'll come for me here while Toni and the kids are gone and I'll be waiting for him."

Wives and children have never been off-limits to killers, in spite of the myth of honor among warriors. Joe was wise to send his family away.

I took South Road through Chilmark. During the summer, the island's roads are filled with cars and bikes, but now they were almost free of traffic and none of the few drivers we saw seemed at all interested in us.

We passed the Chilmark graveyard, site of the island's second most popular tourist attraction: the grave of an entertainer who had taken a shortcut to the afterlife via an overdose of illegal chemical additives. His pilgrim followers still came to meditate and decorate his grave with roaches, roach clips, beer bottles, needles, and other memorabilia. Only the famous bridge on Chappaquiddick attracted more visitors.

I said, "You mentioned five people on the trade mission. Three are dead. That leaves you and one other person. Does that person know about what you think is going on?"

43

"I left a communication, but I don't know if it was needed. Three dead people is a pretty clear message, and like I said, a lot of people in our business are thinking that the Bunny is responsible."

At Bettlebung Corner we took a left. The Chilmark store wasn't doing too much business and the Chocolate Factory was closed. Over us the clear December sky was pale blue. I felt as though an early winter was coming.

Even Quitsa, the loveliest part of the Vineyard, and where I'd live if I had as much money as the island's castle builders, seemed wintery to me. The coldness, I realized, was inside of me, but it seemed to flow out of my eyes and chilled the landscape that was unrolling before us.

As we approached Aquinnah I took note of the slash of white high on a hill north of the road. It was the only visible sign of the huge, mostly underground house where Toni Begay's uncle Bill Vanderbeck now lived with his bride, the widow of a rich man who, after a dangerous life, had died of natural causes, much to the surprise of many people. For the first time I consciously realized that Uncle Bill was, by marriage, a relative of Joe Begay's.

"Maybe you should go live up there with

44

Uncle Bill until all this dust settles," I said. "There's no way anybody can sneak up on that fortress."

"I'm not too proud to do that," said Begay, "but I don't think I need to do it yet, although it might be handy to live with an invisible man."

Uncle Bill Vanderbeck had been considered by his young nieces, Toni and her sister, to be a shaman because he spoke sometimes in amused riddles and because he had the unusual ability of not being seen when he should have been in plain sight. You could be standing there, apparently alone, when suddenly Uncle Bill Vanderbeck would be at your side, seemingly having appeared from nowhere. Uncle Bill claimed it was because he was so insignificant that no one paid any attention to him, but the two little girls had been sure it was because he was a shaman. Now grown up, the sisters still thought so. I'd wondered about it myself.

Joe Begay lived in Aquinnah, in a small neat house just beyond the north end of the famous colored clay cliffs that marked the westernmost point of Martha's Vineyard. During tourist season his wife ran one of the souvenir shops at the top of the cliffs where the tour buses stopped and for years had unloaded elderly visitors who, before shopping, often immediately set off down the hill to the pay toilets, which charged fifty cents a sit.

Because Aquinnah's roads were lined with No Parking signs where once fishermen had parked for free, and because the town parking lot charged an arm and a leg to anyone who wanted to loll on Aquinnah's lovely beaches, I took every opportunity to bad-mouth the town and its politics.

However, recently I had been obliged to abandon one of my favorite complaints: Aquinnah's overpriced pay toilets, which I considered an abomination in the eyes of man and God. For reasons unknown, the town had stopped charging for use of their johns. I had been astonished when I heard the news! Who'd have thunk it?

Maybe there was more civic morality in Aquinnah than I had thought. Maybe someday it would even manifest itself in new parking regulations. Until such time, though, I planned to limit my visits to the town to when I was visiting friends and could park for free in their yards while I fished.

As we approached the Begay driveway, Joe tapped my shoulder. "Why don't you just pull over here and let me out. I'll walk in."

I pulled over. "Better yet," I said, "you get out and I'll drive in. If nobody's there, so much the better. If somebody's waiting for you, I'll play innocent and wonder where you are, then drive out and let you know you have company. It won't be dangerous for me because the Bunny, if he's there, won't have any idea who I am or any reason not to believe me. He can pretend to be a friend in waiting and I'll pretend to believe him. Are you dressed?"

Begay's hand moved and a medium-size pistol appeared in it. "How about you?" he asked.

"I won't need a gun," I said. "I'll just be a guy wondering if you want to try for some cod off the north shore."

He didn't like it but couldn't come up with a reason not to do it. If the Easter Bunny was waiting for him, it would be a nice thing to know.

"If you don't see anybody," he said, "look at the bottom of the front and back doors. I put a bit of cellophane tape between the doors and the frames."

He got out and I drove down his sandy driveway into his yard. Toni's car was there, parked off to the right in its usual place.

I whistled a happy tune as I parked and got out and looked around casually.

Nobody.

I walked to the house and knocked briskly on the door.

No answer.

I looked at the bottom of the door and then knelt and finally saw the cellophane tape still in place between the door and its frame.

I peeked through a window and called Joe's name, then walked around in back of the house and peeked through another window. I called his name again, then knelt in front of the rear door.

The cellophane tape was still there.

As I rose, I heard a small sound and felt cold metal against the back of my neck.

"Put your hands behind your back," said an icy voice, "or I'll blow your spine out through your face."

4

It was a woman's voice, mechanical and cold.

I played innocence assaulted, and trembled as best I could. It wasn't hard. I babbled contradictory ideas together. "Don't shoot! Where are Joe and Toni? I'm not a robber! Take my wallet! Don't kill me! I'll shut my eyes! I won't look at you! Please don't shoot me!" I thrust my hands over my head as I thought a frightened man would do in spite of orders to do otherwise.

The metal pressed harder into my neck.

"Down on your knees. Hands behind your back. Now!"

I got down on my knees and made my voice into a wail. "Who are you? What do you want? My wallet's in my back pocket. The keys are in my car. I won't look at you, I swear!"

"Who are you?"

"J. W. Jackson. I'm a friend of Joe's. My ID's in my wallet. Don't shoot me!"

Fingers fumbled at my back pocket and I wondered if the woman might be distracted by the wallet she removed. But the pressure of the metal didn't lessen.

"Hands behind your back!"

"Jesus! Sure! Anything you say!" I put my hands behind my back. It wasn't a good position from which to attack a person with a gun.

The cold steel against my neck went away and I guessed that the woman had stepped backward, probably carefully beyond any kick I might have in mind, as she went through my wallet.

"Why were you kneeling there at the door? What are you up to?"

I'd anticipated the question. After all, why would any honest, innocent, ordinary person be on his knees staring at the bottom of the locked back door of someone else's house?

"Joe leaves a spare door key down around the back step somewhere. I was looking for it. I couldn't find it. I wanted to leave him a note but I don't have a pen. I wasn't going to rob him, for God's sake! We're friends."

The latter claim might be dangerous

since, if the woman was an enemy of
Joe's — the Easter Bunny herself, perhaps — she might not mind knocking off
one of Joe's friends while she waited for
her real prey to show up. On the other
hand, it was the best excuse I could think
of for my being there and behaving so
oddly; besides, if the woman wasn't the
Easter Bunny or a Bunny cohort, she
might be less inclined to shoot a friend of
Joe's even though she had her suspicions
about me.

In either case, the ice felt thin beneath
my feet. It felt even thinner when her arctic
voice said, "Get on your face and spread
your legs. I'm going to pat you down. If
you give me any grief or if you're carrying
a gun, I'll kill you where you lie."

"Jesus!" I squeaked. "I'm not armed. All
I wanted to do is borrow a pen so I can
leave Joe a note!"

"Shut up. Get down and spread out!"

I did as she said and a moment later the
metal was again pressed against my neck.
It stayed there as a hand began to pass over
me and hook under me. The metal left my
neck suddenly and pressed against my
lower spine, just below the place where a
bullet still snuggled close to my backbone,
a souvenir of my long-passed days on the

Boston PD. My irrational response to the pressure on my lower back was greater fear than when the gun had been on my neck. I lay very still while she ran a fast hand over and between my legs.

The metal left my back. "Roll over very slowly."

I did that, and saw the woman for the first time. She was much younger than I'd imagined. Slim, pale of skin, dark of hair and arctic eye, with high cheekbones and forehead, a firm chin, and wide mouth. A snow queen; an empress of ice. Eurasian, I thought.

From just beyond my best kick she pointed a black semiautomatic pistol at my eyes and said, "Stay spread."

"Yes!" I stretched arms and legs as far apart as they would go and she stepped quickly to me and put the pistol under my chin.

"Don't move."

Her free hand roamed over me, finding my pocketknife, which she tossed aside, and then lingering at my crotch. It wasn't sex; it was a search of a popular spot for a hidden weapon. When she was satisfied that the knife was my only armament, she flowed to her feet and stepped away.

"Sit up. Put your hands behind your neck."

I did that. "Don't shoot me! What do you want?"

"Where's Joe Begay?"

"I don't know. I came here looking for him."

"You're lying!"

"No! Don't shoot me! If I knew where he was I'd tell you. Honest to God. Point that gun somewhere else! Please!"

"Who do you work for?"

"I don't work for anybody! I'm retired! I do odd jobs!" I could hear the exclamation marks in my voice. They were real.

A small movement caught my eye. It was behind her, at the far corner of the house. Joe Begay was peeking around the corner. Then he pointed a long arm at the woman. The hand at the end of the arm held the pistol he'd showed me earlier. I flicked my eyes this way and that, just in case I'd let them linger on Joe a moment too long.

"You only get this one chance," said the woman, straightening her shooting arm. "I don't have time to coddle you. Where is Joe Begay?"

Behind her, Begay cocked his pistol. It was a sound you don't forget when you've heard it once. The woman's body froze in place, but her eyes widened first then were instantly filled with calculation.

"No, don't move," said Begay, as if he could see her face, "don't do anything at all unless I tell you to. Now, drop the gun on the ground." He'd done something with his voice that had changed it in some small way, and I wondered if he did that often in his mysterious line of work.

She hesitated then dropped the pistol.

"That's it," said Begay. "Now, step away. J.W., get the gun."

I did that and Begay said, "Good. Now you can turn."

The woman turned and Begay said, "Well, hello, Kate. Haven't seen you for a while."

"Joe!" The woman stepped toward him and I saw Joe's pistol disappear. She glanced at me and saw her gun in my hand, then looked back at him again. "Joe. I didn't recognize your voice."

"And I wasn't sure that was your back I was looking at. You're a long way from home."

She paused and gestured at me. "Is this man really a friend of yours?"

"He is, but he's not in our line of work. A long time ago we spent a little time to-gether in 'Nam, but now he's a fisherman.

What brings you here, Kate?"

"I need to talk with you in private."

"About what?"

"Something's come up."

"Rabbit ears, by any chance?" I asked.

She looked at me again, then turned back to Joe. "I don't know this guy. Are you sure you do?"

"I know him," said Joe. "Now, Kate, speak up. You can tell J.W. anything you can tell me."

She allowed herself a thin smile. "I'll have to shoot him afterwards, according to the rules."

"Obscenity the rules. Besides, you tried that once and it didn't work."

"Only because of you. You're sure about him?"

"Was Kate part of the trade mission?" I asked Joe.

He nodded and she frowned slightly.

"Yes," he said. "Is that why you're up here?" he asked her.

"The less he knows, the better for everyone," said stubborn Kate. "He can't tell anyone what he doesn't know, and we'll all be safer, including him."

"Maybe, maybe not," said Joe. "He didn't tell you anything but you almost shot him anyway, remember?"

"He was lying," said Kate.

"But you didn't know that."

The fencing made me impatient. "I know about the Easter Bunny," I said to Kate. "I think you must be the other living member of the trade mission. I think you're here because you think it's dangerous to be at home, wherever that may be, and because you want to hook up with Joe in a common front. How did you know where he lives?"

"I told you that some people know," said Joe. "Kate is one of them."

"You trust her."

He shrugged his wide shoulders. "Even in our business you have to trust some people."

I'd have thought that just the opposite would be the general rule; that in the gray and black ops business you'd be better off trusting no one. Or at least not trusting anyone completely.

Still, Kate hesitated.

I could hear the irritation in my voice when I said, "Joe, if your pal here won't talk with me around and if you think she has anything important to say, I'll be on my way. My car is right out there in front of the house."

"Stay," said Joe. "Well, Kate, speak now

or forever hold your peace."

Kate allowed herself a last moment of hesitation, then nodded stiffly. "All right. I don't like it, but maybe you know what you're doing."

"Let's go inside, then," said Joe. "We can chat over a beer, like the old friends we are."

"Fine," I said. I saw my wallet and pocketknife lying on the grass a few feet away and retrieved them. "I'll go check the driveway to see if we have any other visitors, then meet you inside."

5

The beer was actually Ipswich Ale, a brew made north of Boston and favored by Begay. By me, too. There is no bad beer.

We sat in Joe's small living room in front of his fireplace, where kindling and logs had been laid but not lit.

I put Kate's pistol on the coffee table in front of me. She looked at it thoughtfully, then sat down across the table from me.

Now that I could study her when she wasn't aiming that pistol at me, I confirmed that she was indeed a very attractive woman. Midthirties, I guessed, and surely Eurasian. Her up-country fall clothing was formfitting and her boots were good for pavement or forest path. She didn't have a purse, but instead wore a winter coat with pockets aplenty in which she apparently carried her essential gear. Very practical. I wondered if there was a backup pistol somewhere in those clothes.

When we each had a glass in our hands, Joe said, "First, I'd better introduce you two. J.W., this is Kate MacLeod. Kate, this is J. W. Jackson." Kate and I nodded expressionlessly at each other, and Joe looked at Kate. "It's your show," he said.

Her voice had lost its chill and was almost silky. She had a faint accent I couldn't identify. Whatever it was, it triggered a memory, as do certain aromas, of my past, in this case of my brief tour in a long-passed Asian war. Was the accent French? Vietnamese?

"You know about Edo, Francis, and Susan," she said. "Edo's car blew up in Lisbon, Susan OD'd at home, and Francis was collateral damage when somebody robbed his favorite deli just as he was buying himself some kosher salami. Edo was on a job, but Francis and Susan were back in D.C. minding their own business."

"Just as you and I are doing right now," said Joe.

Kate nodded. "When I heard about Susan, my ears perked up because Susan wasn't much of a user; and when I heard about Francis I began to see the Easter Bunny behind every tree."

"He's got other people thinking about him, too," said Joe.

She nodded. "Yes, but none of them was on our trade mission. The building across the street from my apartment has parking in back and a rear entrance, so I moved into a room there where I could see into my own place. I didn't use my own name, of course.

"I left a note on the door of my real apartment to an imaginary maid, rigged the lights to go on and off at reasonable times, and now and then I'd let myself be seen going in or out of my building, although I never actually went back to the apartment.

"After about a week I decided I was paranoid and should stop imagining things, but then I saw a curtain move in my living room. Somebody was in there and was taking a peek outside. It was what I was watching for but it still gave me a jolt."

"I can imagine," said Joe in a gentle voice.

She gave him a small smile. "I watched to see who came out the front door of the building, but nobody unusual did, which meant that whoever had been in my place was still there or had left by the rear door of the building or looked too normal to catch my eye.

"I waited another day, then went over to the apartment. I figured the door wouldn't be booby-trapped because the Easter Bunny probably didn't want to blow up the maid, if there really was a maid. Inside, things looked pretty normal, but I took my time looking around. I don't know if I found everything, but I found enough. Needles beneath the upholstery of the seat cushions in my reading chair and sofa, and another under the bottom sheet of my bed."

"And you figured it was time to leave home for a while," said Joe. "You were right. Did you call the firm? They should be able to sanitize the place while you're gone."

"I haven't called anybody," said Kate. "I came here with the suitcase I'd taken when I moved across the street. Nobody knows I'm not in Bethesda. I figure that if the Bunny comes here after you, he won't be expecting me to be here, too, and that'll give us the edge."

"The apartment has to be cleaned," said Joe. "Even if you never go back to it, some-body else will move in and before that happens, it has to be safe. I'll make a call."

She shook her head. "No, Joe. If you do they'll know I've been in touch with you. It's better if they don't."

He studied her. "You think there's a loose tongue in the firm?"

"I don't want to take the chance. The Bunny's getting his information somewhere."

Joe rubbed his big chin and I heard my voice say, "I'll make the call. To Spitz. He can relay it on to your people."

Kate frowned but Joe nodded. "I know Jake," he said. "That would work."

"Who's Spitz?" asked Kate.

"FBI."

"Jesus!" Her voice was filled with disgust. "FBI? You trust the FBI?"

"I trust Spitz," said Joe.

"You trust this guy, too," said Kate, anger making a snarl of her voice. "You're beginning to have a lot of faith in people, Joe. Maybe it's time you got out of this business."

His smile was small. "I also trust you, Kate."

She sipped her beer, then sighed and shook her head. "Maybe I'm the one who should quit. It's getting too hard to be happy."

"Wait until I kill the Bunny," said Joe.

"Then it'll be safe for you to find another line of work."

That was the second time I heard Joe say he was going to kill the Bunny. During all of the years I'd known him, I'd never heard him mention killing anyone, not even when we were in 'Nam. Even Kate seemed surprised at his words, maybe because people in her line of work prefer to use euphemisms when referring to violent or illegal acts.

"Do you want me to contact Spitz?" I asked Joe.

Joe looked at the woman. "I think it's the thing to do. If J.W. does it, there won't be a direct link to you and me. The Boss won't be surprised to get Spitz's call, because he probably knows by now that you've gone underground."

"I'd prefer to keep it in the firm," said Kate. "Your friend here and this Spitz guy are outsiders."

"You may not have found everything the Bunny left in your apartment," said Joe. "You know what I mean. There may be more needles in the clothes in your closet and bureaus, or in the rugs. Or something may be hooked up to one of your kitchen appliances or your toilet."

"Yes, yes," she said impatiently. "All

63

right, do it your way. Have your friend here call his FBI pal."

"My name's Jackson," I said. "My friends call me J.W."

"I know what your name is," said Kate. "You told me and then I saw your ID when I took your wallet away from you. Remember?"

"How can I forget? When I picked it up I was glad to see that my money was still in it."

"There wasn't much to steal."

"A thief would have to rob me every day for years in order to make any money." I looked at Joe. "What do you want me to tell Spitz?"

Joe gave me a telephone number for Spitz to call, and Kate gave me the address of her apartment in Bethesda, then said, "The message is that the Bunny's been there and left needles where people sit and sleep, and that the cleaners should be very careful. Spitz should say that he doesn't know where I am but that I'm fine. He shouldn't say more."

"I'll tell him that."

"I don't want him to say who called him or from where."

"I guess I'd be jumpy in your place, too," I said. "But you can trust Jake."

"This business can make you sick," she said irritably.

More than one shrink has hypothesized that you have to be at least a little sick to go into the spook business in the first place. Could be, but the same could be said of people who go into a lot of professions, including psychiatry.

"I'll have to go home to make the call," I said. "I don't carry Jake's number around with me."

"As fate would have it," said Joe, "I just happen to know that number." He told me what it was, and looked at Kate. "Now you have it, too," he said. "It may come in handy for you someday. The Bureau may not be on your list of favorite organizations, but Jake Spitz is okay." He handed me his cell phone.

I punched the number and the voice on the other end of the line asked who was calling.

"An old friend of Jake Spitz," I said. "I'd like to talk with him."

"May I give him your name, sir?"

"He can give it to you if he wants to."

"I'm afraid Mr. Spitz isn't available right now. May I take a message and have him get back to you?"

"Tell him it has to do with the Easter Bunny."

"One moment, please."

In less than a moment Jake was on the line. "Spitz here. Steve says you want to talk with me."

"J. W. Jackson here." I gave him Joe's and Kate's message.

"I'll take care of it," said Spitz. "Anything else I can do?"

"Not that I know of. If there's a plan, I haven't been told about it."

"I can guess what it might be," said Spitz. "If you see anyone who might be interested, tell them that the Bunny has engaged the attention of the CI and that the gears are turning down in D.C."

"I'll do that."

I rang off and gave the phone back to Joe. "They've probably traced this call by now," I said.

He shrugged. "They may have traced the call, but they won't know where the phone is. That's the nice thing about short messages on cell phones."

I told them what Spitz had told me.

"Good," said Joe. "Now you can go back home and go scalloping again. Kate and I will take care of the Easter Bunny." He stood up and put out a big hand. "Thank you and good-bye."

I shook the hand, then watched as Kate

reached across the coffee table and picked up her pistol.

She weighed it in her hand, then smiled a strangely warm smile. "How about the bullets? Do I get them back, too?"

"You have a sensitive touch," I said. "Not everybody would have noticed the difference in weight."

"You know how we girls are," she said. "Always conscious of extra ounces."

I dug the bullets out of my pocket and dumped them on the table.

She dropped the magazine out of the pistol and started loading it with bullets. "You're safe," she said, giving me an oddly hungry look. "I'm not going to try to shoot you again."

"Once was enough." I looked at Joe. "You'd better take a good look at Toni's car before you use it. Don't forget that the Bunny likes poisoned needles."

"I'll keep that in mind," said Joe. "If you need me for anything else, let me know."

"I will but I won't. The Bunny is an urban cowboy. He operates in cities. He doesn't know country roads as well as I do. When he comes here he'll be on my turf."

I wondered if Kate was equally at home

on the range or was just wearing country clothes.

"What if he doesn't come here?" I asked. "What if he decides to wait for you to leave the island?"

"He'll come," said Joe. "I've laid out bait he can't refuse."

"What bait is that?"

"Me." Joe smiled a smile that would have frozen Custer's heart. "He'll come." He waved at the door. "Now go home, J.W. If everything goes as it should, Toni and the kids will be back here in a couple of weeks and you won't hear any more about the Easter Bunny."

I normally consider myself to be fairly irresponsible, except for my obligations to my family, but I owed my life to Joe and I didn't like leaving him with only Kate at his right hand.

"Are you sure you don't need some more help?" I asked.

"Kate and I can handle it."

So I went home and when Zee arrived after work at the hospital and was full of questions about Begay, I told her that I'd met Kate, but not how, and what I'd learned about the Easter Bunny. I didn't mention Kate's willingness to shoot me.

When I was through, Zee surprised me by frowning and saying, "I knew other countries had killers working for them, but I didn't know that we do, too."

I thought of a professor I'd once had who told me that he was in the disillusioning business. His students came to his classes with illusions and he helped them shed them. He was not the most popular prof at the university, but he was one of my favorites.

For the next two days I went scalloping with Mike Look out in Cape Pogue Pond.

In Edgartown the scallop season opens around October 1, and for the first month only family permits are allowed. Each scalloper wades out onto the flats with his or her peep sight (known locally as a "Buck Rogers," in honor of the space adventurer who, long ago in the twenty-fifth century, wore a glass-fronted helmet while dodging ray-gun blasts), towing a basket supported by an inner tube, and sporting a long-handled dip net.

The game is to use the peep sight to spot the scallops lying on the pond floor, to dip them up, and to fill the basket. The limit is a bushel a week per permit. On a good day, you can get your limit in half an hour. On a bad one you can get skunked. On a lovely, sunny, windless day, you can scallop in a T-shirt and you're in heaven; on a cold, windy one, with waves splashing icy water over the tops of your waders, you freeze your bippies.

At the end of the month the professionals get to go to work. Their tools are a boat with a culling board and a number of drags, and they can work in deep water beyond the reach of the waders. They put out the drags and pull them along the bottom until they think they're full, then winch them in and dump them on the culling board.

They keep the scallops and shove everything else back overboard — the seaweed, the rocks, the conchs, the broken shells, the pieces of junk, and the rusty tin cans. They toss broken glass and bottles into a waste barrel, put out the drags again, and repeat the process. When the scalloping is good, a man can make a lot of money, but winter scalloping is a wickedly cold way to make a living, and late in the season, just before spring, the pickings are thin and life is even harder. But for Mike and me, it wasn't spring yet. There were a lot of scallops and we did well. The deer hunters did equally well ashore, and in the papers, letters from the VETA people boiled with moral outrage.

Then, three days after I'd brought Joe home from the Cape, I saw Kate in the Bunch of Grapes bookstore in Vineyard Haven when I went in for the latest Bill Tapply novel. She was reading a white-jacketed book in the biography section and not paying much attention to her fellow customers.

One of them, however, was paying attention to her. He was a slender man in his thirties, wearing a stylish green winter coat and a felt hat decorated with a little feather in the headband. He was pretending to browse but he was really keeping an eye on Kate while she read. When she finally decided not to buy the book she was examining and went out into the street, he followed her.

I put down my book and went after him. He was about twenty feet behind her when I brushed past him and said, "Kate! How nice to see you!"

She turned like a cat, one hand thrusting into a coat pocket. Behind me I heard the sound of scurrying feet. I turned and saw the man in the green coat trot away across the street, dodge a car, and disappear down toward the Stop and Shop parking lot.

I turned back and Kate was staring at me with feral eyes, her hand still in her coat pocket.

6

"Was that him?" I asked. "Was that the Easter Bunny?"

She was angry. "What are you doing here? Why are you following me?"

Anger begets anger. I tried to repress my own. "I'm not following you, but that guy was. I was in the store to buy a book. Did you see him? Did you recognize him? And stop pointing that damned pistol at me!"

She took her hand from her pocket.

"You're getting careless," I said. "He was watching you in the bookstore and he was right behind you on the sidewalk when I called to you. Well, did you see him? Do you know who he is?"

She shook her head. "I only saw his back. I didn't recognize him."

"Because you were really looking at me instead of at him."

"What if I was? What difference does it

make? I don't know what the Bunny looks like. That could have been him but it may have been an innocent bystander."

He hadn't looked so innocent to me, but maybe he was just a guy hot for a beautiful woman. Maybe he'd gone after her to hit her up for a date.

"I'm not your enemy," I said. "You've got to get that idea out of your head and open your eyes to other people who might be. First you got lost in that book you were reading and then you stayed lost right here on the street. Your mind was somewhere else when it should have been focused on why you came here to the Vineyard."

She looked up and down the sidewalk. It was a chilly day and there weren't too many people nearby, although I recognized one woman coming toward us. "I needed a break," Kate said. "Joe and I have been up there in the woods too long. Nothing's happened. I'm a city girl. I need some entertainment. I'm getting claustrophobic."

Boredom has probably done in a lot of people. They get twitchy and leave their safe places and go out into the world, where they get into trouble. I offered Kate that opinion.

She frowned, then nodded. "You're right, but this waiting is getting on my

74

nerves. The damned Easter Bunny is taking his time getting here."

"He may already be here," I reminded her. "That may have been him just now. Did you see the guy's face at all? Would you know him again?"

"No. How about you?"

"I'll know him. I saw him watching you in the store."

At that moment the woman I'd recognized coming down the street stopped in front of me, thrust her angry face up toward mine, and said, "Murderer!"

I bowed. "Nice to see you, too, Mrs. Quackenbush."

The woman said, "Humph," glared, and walked on up the street.

Kate looked at her back. "What on earth was that all about?"

"That's Irma Quackenbush," I said. "She's president of VETA, Vineyarders for the Ethical Treatment of Animals. She hates everyone who eats meat." I explained what VETA was all about.

"I've heard of those people," said Kate, "but this is the first one I've actually seen. Are they all like her?"

"No, Irma is an extreme case. I think the only thing that keeps her from shooting hunters and fishermen is that we're animals, too. Someday, though, she may change her mind about that."

The VETA fanatics are pretty closely related to all the other fanatics who think they alone are righteous. I consider such moralists to be far more dangerous than professional terrorists like the Easter Bunny, who kill for money, plain and simple. You can reason with a professional shootist but you can't reason with an Irma Quackenbush.

But I wasn't thinking about Irma and her fanatic friends, I was wondering what had really brought Kate to Martha's Vineyard and now into Vineyard Haven, which is as far from Joe's house in Aquinnah as you can get and still be on the island. Her emotions had seemed a bit out of whack from the beginning, and still did.

First, she'd almost shot me for no good reason. Even after seeing my ID and finding no weapons on me, and having no reason to believe I was other than I said I was, I thought she still would have pulled the trigger. Pro assassins, one of which she apparently was, generally don't kill people unnecessarily because, if for no other reason, any killing attracts attention and attention is the last thing they want. Whenever someone deliberately commits a public killing, you know you're dealing with an amateur or a professional politician who wants the publicity. All of the martyrs who willingly die for the Cause are amateurs. Their leaders, on the other hand, may be very professional. They never die if they can help it. Their job is to get the amateurs to do the glorious killing and dying.

Kate was supposedly a professional, but her raw emotions when she'd ambushed me were inconsistent with that persona.

And those emotions had only changed when Joe Begay had insisted that I was to be trusted, and she had acquiesced. Or seemed to.

And now, three days later, here she was in Vineyard Haven, paying no attention to her surroundings even though she knew that the Easter Bunny was seeking her and might already be on the island. It wasn't the sort of move a trained professional agent would make. Allowing yourself to be distracted in a war zone is the act of an amateur.

"What were you thinking about, anyway?" I asked.

She lifted her chin. "None of your business."

"You may be right. Are you staying up at Joe's?"

"None of your business."

"Right again, I guess. Do you have a car?"

"I have transportation."

"Where is it?"

She hesitated, then nodded toward the town parking lot. "Down there. Don't try to be protective. I've got my eyes open now."

On the bright side, my old Toyota was parked in that lot, too. On the dark side, that's where the man in the green coat had been headed when last seen.

"Your mind isn't on your work," I said. "I suggest that you get out of this town. I'll walk you to your car and make sure no one follows you when you leave."

She sniffed a ladylike sniff, but a sniff nevertheless. "And just how will you do that?"

"By following him in my own car if he follows you, and making sure he knows I'm there. I doubt if the Bunny wants to be caught between two enemy cars. I think he'll drop the tail."

She almost rolled her eyes. "Ye gods! You're not armed and you're not trained for this work. You're more a danger to me and yourself than to him."

I nodded. "Maybe. But he doesn't know

that. I might be the second coming of James Bond, as far as he's concerned."

"Ha!" But she was sweeping the street with her eyes. "All right, let's go. I've already made an idiot of myself once. I can't afford to do it again."

"We're just old friends who happened to bump into each other," I said. "Come on, we'll walk down to the parking lot. Did you notice that the police station fronts on the lot? A gambling man might think that was a plus for our side."

"I did notice that. I parked as near to the station as I could get."

We crossed the street and walked down the alley beside the movie theater. As we went, I was looking for the man, and when we came into the parking lot I put a hand on Kate's arm and stopped her while I surveyed the lot for sign of him.

He wasn't in sight and we went on to Kate's car, which turned out to be a rental. I wondered if the Easter Bunny had followed her into town and knew what she was driving. I asked her.

"No one followed me," she said coolly. "I know how to spot a tail and there wasn't any."

"The guy was with you in the bookstore," I said.

"He might have been an ordinary guy on the make."

I suspected that she'd had experience with such guys.

"My truck is right down there between here and the street," I said. "You pull out and I'll wave bye-bye. If anyone follows you, I'll be on him like ugly on an ape before you get out of town."

"You islanders have quaint turns of phrase," said Kate. She got into the driver's seat, backed out of the parking place, and drove away. I waved a friendly good-bye and watched her go out of sight in front of the brand-new Stop and Shop. No one followed her. No one even looked her way.

I waited awhile and then walked back up to Main Street and went into the bookstore. I looked around and didn't see the mystery man anywhere, then went over to the biography section. After a while I found the book that I thought Kate had been reading. It was a biography of a woman whose passions and scandalous affairs had made her name notorious and had kept her in the international society columns for most of her life.

I put the book back on the shelf.

Hmmmmm. Could it be? Was Kate in

love with Joe Begay? It would account for her rush to the Vineyard to be with him in a time of danger; it would account for her willingness to shoot me just in case I wasn't who I said I was but was really the Bunny or a Bunny accomplice; and it would account for her distraction and her need to get away from Aquinnah if, during their three weeks together, Joe, who I knew loved his wife and children, had shown no romantic interest in her.

So maybe the beautiful assassin was infatuated. If so, she was in trouble. And so was Joe, if he was depending on her, because love intrudes on cold thought, and cold thought was what was needed to deal with the Easter Bunny.

I turned toward the door and as I did so I saw the man across the street, looking at the store. As if he spotted me looking back at him, he turned and walked away. There was a pretty good crowd in the store, and by the time I got past them and into the street, he was gone. I ran down to the parking lot but he wasn't in sight.

Uncle Bill Vanderbeck would have known how he performed that disappearing act, but I didn't. I wondered if the man was watching me even though I couldn't see him. I felt as I sometimes had when I was a kid and it was night and my bedroom was dark, and something seemed to be lurking in that far corner. It could see me but I couldn't see it. My only hope was to lie so quiet and still that it wouldn't notice me under the covers.

Here and now I couldn't hide and try to hold my breath, so I got into the Land Cruiser and started home. About a mile out of town I noticed a black car behind me. I slowed down; so did the car. I speeded up; so did the car.

Trouble at River City.

7

I took a right at the new four-way stop sign and drove toward the airport. Behind me, the black car did the same. I cut left on the road leading to the state forest headquarters, and then went left again onto the road that led back to the regional high school.

By this time the driver of the car realized that I knew he was tailing me. He pulled into sight behind me but then stopped and got out of his car. In my rearview mirror I saw that he was wearing a green coat and a felt hat. He lifted binoculars to his eyes.

Blast and drat! I slammed on the brakes and slid to a stop with the Toyota sideways in the road. Back toward forest headquarters the driver lowered his glasses, got back into his car, made a U-turn, and drove out of sight. I grabbed my own binoculars but before I could adjust them the car was gone.

I tossed the glasses aside and turned and followed the car, but by the time I got back to the airport road it was nowhere to be seen.

Not good, Kemo Sabe. It was possible that the guy had not gotten my license plate number, but I doubted that and I definitely hadn't gotten his, so he had the edge.

Spilt milk. I drove on home. There was no one in my mirror, but that didn't make any difference. It wasn't hard to trace a license plate to its owner.

Zee was still at the ER and the kids were in school. Only the cats, Oliver Underfoot and Velcro, were at home. I checked their food and water then got John Skye's house keys and drove to Oak Bluffs, where I loaded up on groceries at the Reliable Market before driving on to John Skye's farm.

John and Mattie Skye generally summered on the island, but they wintered in Weststock while he taught at the college there. Their twin daughters, Jill and Jen, whom I'd known since they were tots, were now college women at Weststock. I'd never been able to tell them apart, but both of them were cute and full of zip and hormones and had no shortage of young men in their lives, which meant no shortage of worries for their parents. Because John and the twins would be busy in class until the Christmas holidays, they wouldn't be using their Edgartown house for a while.

Which meant that I could.

The Skyes' old farm was off the Edgartown–West Tisbury road, a few miles from my place. The house, barn, outbuildings, and corrals were in good shape, and it was my job to look after them over the winter. Today, though, I was interested in turning the thermostat up, making up beds in three bedrooms, and putting food in the fridge. When things were ready, I went home again, keeping an eye on my rearview mirror, but seeing no black car or any other suspicious-looking vehicle.

I was not happy. I had gotten involved in something that wasn't really any of my business. Joe Begay had asked me to stay out of it, and I'd planned to do just that, but now I was back in it again. The man in the green coat was not only interested in Kate, but knew that I had some sort of connection with her. And now he knew or would soon know who I was and where I lived.

Which meant that my family was now possibly in danger. Joe, who understood how violent the Easter Bunny could be, had sent his family out to Oraibi. I would move mine to John Skye's house, just in case the Bunny decided to include them in his plans. Zee was not going to like it, but she would go there because of the children.

Are there any times that do not try men's souls? There are, but this wasn't one of them.

When Zee got home from work and heard my tale, she was as upset as I'd guessed she would be.

"You told me you weren't getting involved in this. You told me Joe wants to handle it himself!"

"I wasn't, and he does. But things happen. I just want you and the kids to be safe. I'll be over there with you. It'll just be for a few days."

"You don't know that. And what if Joe doesn't stop him? What then? What if something happens to Joe and to this woman, this Kate? Then what?"

"Then it'll be over."

"And this Easter Bunny will go back home and blow up more people just like before! Is that it?"

"Nothing's going to happen to Joe."

"But what if it does? What if something

goes wrong? This Easter Bunny is a professional killer!" She paused, frowned, and then said, "Are you telling me that Joe is one, too? That Joe and this Kate MacLeod woman are killers, too? Is that what you're saying?"

I felt my hand rub my chin. "He never said so in so many words."

"But that's what you think, isn't it? My God! Joe Begay. I wonder if Toni knows."

I put my hands on her shoulders. "Look," I said. "Joe's work takes him to some hard places. He may have done things that most of us wouldn't do or couldn't do. I don't know about that and neither do you. What I do know is that he saved my life a long time ago and that he's been my friend since he moved to the island and that I trust him. And so can you."

She took a deep breath and then nodded and put her arms around me and laid her head against my chest.

"Yes. I know you're right. And before you say it, I'll say it: not all killings are the same. I know that."

She stepped back. "All right, we'll move over to John's place until this business is ended. Let's pack the stuff the kids will need."

"Does that include the computer?" Our new computer was still pretty much a mystery to me, but it seemed to be a necessity to Joshua and Diana, who used it for schoolwork and, to a lesser extent, for fun and games.

"Yes," said Zee, "that includes the computer. In fact, if they know we're taking the computer, the kids will realize that this isn't just an adventure but that they'll have to study just as hard at John's house as they do here. It'll get them into the right frame of mind."

We packed suitcases and the computer into Zee's little red Jeep.

"What about Oliver and Velcro?"

"They can stay here," I said. "I'll come over every day and make sure they're fed and that the cat flap is open in the morning and closed in the evening so they'll have to stay inside for the night."

"Good. I don't want some raccoon to bite one of my kitties."

"They're not kitties," I said. "They're grown-up cats."

"They're kitties to me," said Zee.

Kitties. Why do people speak about babies and other little animals in diminutive terms and talk to them in high-pitched voices?

When everything else was in the car, Zee retrieved the key from the top of the gun case and opened the door. Inside were my father's .30-'06 and shotguns. Inside, too, were the old .38 Police Special I'd carried as a Boston cop before semiautomatic pistols came into vogue, and Zee's two guns: the little Beretta 380 that she used when Manny Fonseca first taught her to shoot, and the modified 1911 model Colt .45 she now used in pistol competition. For pacifistic Zee, somewhat to her surprise and chagrin, was, in Manny's terms, a natural, by which he meant she could shoot rings around most people, including me. She had the pistol competition trophies to prove it and she was getting better with each passing day.

Now, as I watched, she took the Beretta and a box of ammunition out of the case and put them in her purse. Then she shut and locked the door and returned the key to its place. I said nothing. She looked at me. I still said nothing.

"Just in case," she said.

I nodded, but said, "I don't think you'll need it."

"I don't think so either, but you know what Manny says."

"Yes, I do."

Manny was fond of the shootist's maxim, It's better to have a gun and not need it than to need it and not have it.

I could understand that because I felt the same way about beer.

When Joshua and Diana came down our long, sandy driveway after their day in school, we told them about our plans to live at the farm for a few days.

"It'll be like a secret adventure," I said, sitting on my heels in front of them. "I don't want you to tell anyone about it until we come back to our house."

Joshua, ever a romantic, thought that sounded fine. Diana, however, was more practical. "What about Oliver Underfoot and Velcro? Are they coming, too?"

"No, I'll come over here every day and take care of them."

"But they'll miss us."

"I'll spend some time with them every day. Besides, we won't be staying at the farm very long."

"How long?"

"Just a few days."

"What about our computer? We need our computer for school."

As is often the case, what was once a luxury had become a necessity, but I had neither the time nor the inclination to philosophize upon that very common phenomenon.

"We're taking it with us," I said. "It's already in the car. We'll set it up in John's library."

"That sounds good," said Joshua. "I like the library. I like all those books." What a bright little chap. Like father, like son.

Diana thought for a moment, then negotiated. "Can I sleep in Jill's bedroom, Pa? I can see the barn from her window."

"Sure."

She smiled. "Okay, then. Let's go."

And we did. Zee and the kids rode in Zee's Jeep. I waited at the end of our driveway until they went over a hill toward Edgartown and out of sight. No black car followed them. Then I turned the other way, toward Vineyard Haven, and took the long way to the farm via the airport road. No one followed me either.

So far, so good. But I was jumpy.

The next morning, I took the kids to school, explained to the woman in the office that either Zee or I would be delivering and picking them up for a few days, then went back to our house. Everything looked normal outside as I walked around the building. The pieces of cellophane tape I'd put at the foot of the front and back doors were still in place. I went inside and was met by loud meows from Oliver Underwood and Velcro. I opened the cat flap and they both immediately went out. So much for my cats missing me.

I filled their food and water dishes, then got our cell phone out of the truck and called Joe Begay's house.

He didn't answer.

8

I got an answering machine with Toni Begay's voice. I wasn't surprised that Joe wasn't home, but I'd have been happier if he had been, since that would have suggested that he felt secure in the house, which in turn would have suggested that the Bunny problem had been resolved, probably with extreme prejudice.

However, I wasn't totally out of Joe's loop because I'd noted his cell phone number when I'd talked to Jake Spitz, so I dialed that phone. While it was ringing I wondered if the phone was one of those that told you who was calling so you could decide whether or not you wanted to answer. I'd read about such phones and about other modern electronic devices that allow you to stay in constant touch with others, but little of it had registered with me because I generally prefer not to be in touch, and usually only carried our cell phone when we were cruising the far Chappy beaches, in case the Jeep broke down in some obscure place.

When Joe finally answered, I told him I was on my own cell phone and asked him if he considered this to be a secure line.

"Cell phones are not secure," he said. "People with bombs can drop them on you if you use your cell phone too much because they can zero in on where you are."

"Now that you mention it," I said, "I remember reading about that happening in the latest Gulf War. They rocketed a caravan of cars going across the desert because some wanted guy was talking on his cell phone while they drove."

"Right," said Joe. "I don't recall if they got the right guy, but they got somebody. Anyway, I don't expect any rocket attacks on Martha's Vineyard, but if you want a secure line you should use a regular phone that you know hasn't been tapped. Why do you ask? Do you have something to say that other people shouldn't hear?"

"I thought I'd let you decide that."

"Why don't you meet me at Uncle Bill's old place?"

A good suggestion. If the Bunny was actually listening in, he'd be hard-pressed to know who Uncle Bill was or where he'd once lived. "I'll be there," I said.

Uncle Bill Vanderbeck, who now lived in the mostly underground mansion belonging to his new wife, still owned his old place off Lighthouse Road in Aquinnah. His house, like many, was at the end of a sandy driveway. It was a well-maintained old farmhouse with weathered gray shingles and gray trim. There was a small barn behind it that he'd used as a garage for his elderly car, and on the far side of the yard was a vegetable garden that was now hors de combat for the year, although it had the look of having been well tended during the growing season.

No surprise there, since Uncle Bill was a locally famous gardener as well as a rumored shaman. Bill scoffed at the latter idea, but the shaman stories didn't go away, maybe because reputations are hard to shake or maybe because the idea of a shaman living on Martha's Vineyard was just too interesting to give up. I liked it myself, in fact. I also liked the idea of the Loch Ness monster, of course.

I drove up to Dodgers Hole and took the road that led through to the West Tisbury road. There are people living in those developments who want to put up gates to stop through traffic such as mine, but so far they have not prevailed.

No one seemed to be following me, so I turned right toward the airport and drove on to Aquinnah. Here and there, beside the road, were the parked cars and pickups of deer hunters who had managed to find some of the increasingly rare woods where people could still hunt.

Like the beaches that had in my youth been open to fishermen but were now behind the locked gates of rich new land-owners who kept their shorefronts to themselves, woodlands once open to hunters were now behind similar gates and the trees beside roadsides were covered with No Trespassing signs. I once counted over a hundred such signs along North Road alone, and there were probably more that I missed because I had to keep an eye on the road as I counted. Some of the signs were only twenty or thirty feet apart and I could see a half dozen of them at the same time. As always they made me wonder about the psyches of the people who had posted them.

Frost had been right about walls and I was sure he'd have similar thoughts about those signs. Zee and I had no such signs on our land, and the worst thing that had ever happened as a result was mild shock to those drivers who explored our driveway and happened to come into our yard while Zee and I were lying in our lounges perfecting our all-over tans. Without exception, the drivers all turned around and fled.

My trip to Aquinnah took me through the Quitsa section of Chilmark, which, looking out on Noshaquitsa Pond, is the loveliest part of Martha's Vineyard any time of year. The only beauty it lacks is the sight of the big schooners such as you find in the Vineyard Haven Harbor. Aside from that, and the fact that it's twenty miles from the nearest liquor store, Quitsa is pretty close to perfect, and once again as I drove through I decided that it's the place I'd live if I had my druthers and an unlimited amount of money.

An added attraction to the area is the Quitsa Quoit, a small stone structure that consists of a flat capstone supported by several short standing stones. It looks like a miniature version of the prehistoric quoits found throughout the British Isles and in other places in Western Europe, and is the subject of radically different theories about its origins.

The three principal such theories are

that it was built by pre-Columbian European visitors, that it was built by native Indians, and that it was built by European farmers some time after they came to the island in the seventeenth century. Just why any of these groups would have gone to all the effort of building the quoit is unknown, although there are also theories about that.

I have no theory about the quoit but I am fond of it nevertheless and sneak in to see it sometimes when no one seems to be looking.

That morning I passed on without stopping and drove to Uncle Bill's house.

There I found two vehicles in the yard: Uncle Bill's ancient Ford and the rental car I'd last seen driven by Kate MacLeod. I considered the possibilities of this small fleet as I walked to the house.

Joe Begay opened the door before I got to it and waved me inside. The smell of bacon was in the air, and the breakfast dishes were stacked in the drying rack beside the sink. Kate was seated at the kitchen table with *The New York Times* spread out before her. She looked scrubbed and younger than when I'd last seen her.

I accepted a cup of coffee and joined her

and Joe at the table.

"Well?" said Joe.

I looked at Kate. "Did you tell him what happened in Vineyard Haven?"

His dark eyes flicked to her face and she met his gaze so calmly that I was sure she'd anticipated my question when she'd heard I was coming.

"No," she said. "I'm sorry, Joe. I probably should have told you, but I wasn't sure that it meant anything. I'm still not sure."

"Tell me now," said Joe. There was no rancor in his voice but his eyes seemed to glow.

She told him about the man in the green coat, and about meeting me, and about driving out of town without a tail. "It's possible that he was just a guy hoping to pick me up," she said. "Maybe he went away because J.W. got to me first and knew my name."

"Maybe," said Joe. "You're an attractive woman. A lot of men would be drawn to you."

She colored slightly and I wondered again if she wished he were one of those men. Then I wondered if, perhaps, he actually was, since many a happily married man has had a fling with another woman.

But when I looked at Joe's face I saw no sign of affection there, only a thoughtful expression.

"There's more to the story," I said, and told them about seeing the man again, across from the bookstore, then about spotting the black car behind me, and then about the episode on the road in the state forest. "He may have gotten my license plate number," I said. "If he did, he probably knows who I am and where I live."

Joe frowned. "Have you told Zee?"

"I've moved her and the kids out of the house for the time being. I went back home this morning. There was no sign of anybody having been there."

"With luck, your family won't have to be away from home for long." Joe looked back at Kate. "I think we can be pretty sure that your admirer wasn't just interested in a hot date with you. You'd better stay put here for a while until we figure out who he is and what he wants. Describe him for me."

She shook her head. "I only saw his back as he was crossing the street. Medium height, slim, forest-green winter coat, soft hat. I didn't see his face. He walked fast and he was out of sight very quickly." She looked at me. "You saw more of him than I did."

I nodded. "Clean-shaven; brownish hair, I don't know how long or short because his collar was turned up and his hat was pulled down. I couldn't tell his eye color. Straight nose in a thin face. Very average and forgettable. He was pretending to read a novel but he was really watching Kate. That's why I noticed him. If I hadn't known her, I wouldn't have given him a second glance."

Joe sipped his cooling coffee. "Sound like anybody you know, Kate?"

"I know a lot of forgettable men."

Begay smiled. "If he is one of the bad guys," he said to her, "how did he find you?"

She spread her hands. "I can't guess. At home I hang out in bookstores more than most but the Bunny probably wouldn't know that, and even if he did I doubt if he'd plant himself in the Bunch of Grapes and wait for me to come in, especially since there's no way he could know I'm even on the island."

"Who does know you're here?" I asked.

She gave me a cool glance. "You do."

I ignored her sarcasm. "Who else besides Joe and me?"

"If your friend Spitz is as smart as you and Joe think he is, he may have figured it out."

"I don't think Jake would tell the Bunny," I said. "Did you tell anyone where you were going when you left Bethesda?"

"No!"

"You didn't tell your boyfriend?"

She snapped a look at me. "I don't have a boyfriend at the moment!"

I smiled. "How about a girlfriend?"

She didn't smile back. "I have women friends, but I don't have a girlfriend!"

"You like men, but you don't have a boyfriend. That's hard to believe. Like Joe says, you're a very attractive woman. I imagine you could have your pick of men."

Her eyes flicked to and from Joe, then came back to me. "You'd be wrong. Besides, I never told anyone at all that I was coming here!"

"No friend, no brother, no mother, no lover?"

"No!"

"No trusty ex-beau who loves you even though now you're just friends?"

"No! Now get out of my private life!" Her voice was angry and her eyes were hot, but there was an odd excitement in her face.

I looked at Begay. "How about you, Joe? You plan to deal with the Bunny right here on the island, so you must have told somebody where he could find you."

Joe's eyes were hooded. "If I did, I didn't mention Kate. My plans were made before I found her pointing that pistol at your head. Kate shouldn't be here but she is and now she's got somebody on her tail. It complicates things."

"Send her away," I said. "Put her on a plane and fly her out of here. The Bunny won't be able to follow her and be here with you at the same time."

"I'm not going anywhere!" said Kate.

"Where should I send her?" asked Joe. "Back to Bethesda and more poisoned pins? No, we've talked about it and she's staying right here in this house with me. Uncle Bill says we can use the place as long as we need it."

"She sounds like more trouble than she may be worth."

He shook his head. "You're wrong. She's a trained agent and we've worked well together in the past. She's good at what she does, and she makes two of us against one Bunny." He looked at her and so did I. Her expression suggested gratitude and pleasure. Then he looked back at me. "You're the problem, J.W.," he said. "I've gotten you involved in this business and I don't know how to get you out."

9

"So far I don't think I'm in trouble," I said. "All Green Coat knows about me is that I know Kate. If he checks up on me, that's still all he'll know. I'm just a local guy with a family. The more he checks, the less reason he'll have to think I'm anything else."

"Fine," said Joe. "Then go back to your family and leave the Bunny to Kate and me. It'll be over pretty quickly, I think. When it is, I'll get a message to you on your cell phone and you can take your family home again."

"And later you'll tell me the whole story."

He smiled. "Sure I will."

I smiled back. "Sure you will." I looked at Kate. "Since I may not see you again, there's one thing you can tell me: How'd you get your last name?"

"Why do you ask?"

"You don't look like a Celt. Besides, I like to know a little something about people who try to kill me."

She shrugged. "My father is an engineer. A wandering Scot. He met my mother while he was building a railroad in Indochina. I'm the result. But I didn't try to kill you. If I had, you'd be dead. I was deciding whether to do it when Joe, here, showed up."

"Joe makes a habit of saving my hide," I said. I shook hands with him, nodded to her, and went out to my truck. As I drove down-island I checked my rearview mirrors. No one was following me.

Maybe Green Coat didn't need to follow me around anymore because he knew where I lived and figured he could wait for me there. Or maybe he'd managed to stick an electric tracking device on my car and could find me whenever he wanted.

Or maybe he'd decided I wasn't a danger to him and didn't merit further attention.

I wondered if he was the Easter Bunny.

If not, who was he and why was he interested in Kate MacLeod?

Was he, after all, just a guy anxious to jump her lovely bones? If so, why follow me?

I was long on questions and short on answers. One thing I was pretty sure of was that if Joe Begay did terminate the Bunny, I'd never learn where or how and nobody outside of his professional circle would even know it had happened. The Bunny would simply be gone.

On the other hand, if the Bunny killed Joe and Kate, there was a good chance that he'd make a spectacle of his work, to show people who cared about such things that he was more than capable of tough jobs that others in his field might shun and that he was not a man to mess with. It would be good publicity and could lead to a fee hike for his services.

I wondered why no one had a good photo of him. He must have passport pictures, at least. Why didn't Joe's agency have a copy? Some agency must have one; why didn't the members of the fatal trade mission have copies?

I was glad to be out of the Bunny business, but I wasn't sure that was actually the case. I might think I was, and Joe and Kate might think I was, but the Bunny might not think so and Green Coat might not think so and maybe there were other people I didn't even know about who didn't think so. And if any of them didn't think so, I might be a target.

Good grief! I was getting paranoid! Pretty soon I'd be hearing voices and thinking that everybody in the whole world was a Bunny!

Maybe I was paranoid and being followed at the same time.

Maybe this, maybe that. Maybe, maybe, maybe.

Maybe nothing at all.

As I passed a parked pickup, two hunters in orange camouflage coats and caps came out of the woods. One carried two shotguns and the other had a deer slung over his shoulder. They looked tired but happy. I'd once been a hunter so I knew how they felt. There'd be venison for their supper tonight. My mouth grew moist at the thought.

For them, life was good and the Easter Bunny didn't exist.

I thought of the torturer's horse and of the boy falling from the sky while the ship sailed calmly by. The world didn't stop turning for love or for loss. It had turned as Abelard and Héloïse lay abed, it had turned as Rome fell, and it would turn the day they buried me.

In my mind an image appeared of the wheels of my truck turning on the turning earth. It was a hint that I was wasting time thinking shallow thoughts. Enough of that! I had most of the day left, so I'd do something useful for a change. I decided to go home, get keys for the houses I looked after during the winter, and put in a few hours of caretaking.

But, just in case, I was careful when I drove down our long, sandy driveway. I checked the woods on both sides, drove slowly, and eased into the yard. Nothing seemed unusual. Oliver Underfoot and Velcro ran to meet me, giving me their usual lectures. I studied the house, then got out and petted the cats.

The tape was still at the bases of the front and back doors, so I went inside and checked the rooms. Everything looked the same as when I'd left it earlier that morning.

I got the keys and was walking toward the front door when I heard a car coming down the driveway. I looked out a window. It was a black sedan.

I tossed the keys onto a table and trotted to the gun cabinet. I hurriedly opened it and loaded my old .38 revolver while listening for the silence that would follow the sedan's engine stopping and the sound of the driver's door shutting behind him.

But the engine didn't stop and the car door didn't close. I went back to the window. The car had stopped beside my truck. The man in the green coat was only partially out of the car and was sagging against the door as if he was too tired to go farther.

As I looked, he lurched to his feet and staggered toward the house, and I saw blood on the front of his coat and the hand that he held against his chest.

I shoved the pistol in my belt and ran out of the house to meet him. He put out his other hand, reaching toward me. His knees let go as I got to him, and I caught him as he fell.

"Take it easy," I said. "I'll call nine-one-one!"

I started to rise, but he grasped my coat and stared into my face. His mouth was full of blood, and when he tried to speak the sound was lost in red bubbles. He turned his head and spat out the blood then again looked up at me. I put my ear near his mouth and he said in a very distant voice, "Not the Bunny. Tailgate."

Just those four words, and then he left his body behind and went wherever the dead go next.

I looked down at him. His still-open eyes

were blue, I now saw, and his hair was brown and cut fairly short. A nice-looking guy in an average sort of way. He wore a wedding ring and a gold wristwatch that had cost a lot more than mine. You should never pay more than nine dollars for a wristwatch. The expensive ones don't keep time any better and they get lost or broken just as often.

I unzipped his coat, then went into the house, washed the blood off my hands, and put on a pair of the disposable rubber gloves we keep in a box under the sink. Back at the body I avoided as much of the blood as possible while I found the man's wallet in a breast pocket and a flat black semiautomatic pistol in a belt holster. The wallet held money, credit cards, a photo of a young woman and two children, a driver's license, and some business cards. The license had his photo and his name and address. Samuel Arbuckle had lived in Alexandria, just outside Washington. The business cards gave his name, phone number, e-mail address, and profession. According to the cards, Sam had worked for the Defense Intelligence Agency.

Hmmmmm.

I had read about the DIA. It was the Pentagon's private spy outfit, meant to provide it with better intelligence than it was getting from the CIA. It not only conducted its own analysis of data, it had its own agents, including spies, counterspies, and other human assets.

I went through Sam's pockets but found only the usual stuff. No magic decoding ring or cyanide pill. In an inside coat pocket I did find his official DIA ID card.

I kept one of the business cards but put everything else back where I found it. Then I zipped up Sam's coat and went to the car and shut off the engine. A window sticker identified it as a rental car from an island agency. There was a smear of blood on the side of the car just behind the driver's door.

I went inside the house, buried the gloves in the trash container under the sink, and called 911.

The EMs, the Edgartown Police, and an ambulance got there almost at the same time. Tony D'Agostine of the Edgartown PD spoke to me, looked at the body, and called Sergeant Dom Agganis of the state police, because in Massachusetts, except for Boston, which has its own homicide detectives, the state cops are in charge of all murder investigations.

Dom arrived with Officer Olive Otero,

with whom I did not get along and who didn't like me either.

"I should have known you'd be involved," she said as she looked at me. "Covered with blood and standing over a dead body. At least we don't have to figure out who did it. I'll take that pistol."

I'd forgotten the pistol in my belt. I dug it out and handed it to her.

"My gun hasn't been fired, and the man died in my arms," I said to Dom, ignoring Olive. "I'd like to take a shower and get into some clean clothes."

"Later," said Dom.

"We'll need the medical examiner to make it official," said an EM, coming up to us, "but I'd say the deceased died from an acute case of lead poisoning."

Dom nodded and looked at me. "Who is he?"

"I don't know," I lied. "I was inside when he drove down here. He tried to make it into the house but this is as far as he got. He died pretty fast. I turned the car engine off and called nine-one-one. The car's a local rental, so he's probably from off-island."

Another police car came down the driveway and parked. Policemen with cameras and evidence bags got out. They said hello to Dom and began to look around and take pictures.

"See if he's got any ID on him," said Dom to Olive. "Wear a pair of rubber gloves."

"Yes, sir," said Olive.

"And put that gun in an evidence bag."

"Yes, sir." Olive was all business.

"Now," said Dom, "if you don't know this guy, why do you suppose he drove down here so he could die in your front yard?"

10

"I don't know why he came here," I said.

"He say anything?"

"Yes. Four words. He said, 'Not the Bunny. Tailgate.' "

Dom stared at me. "That's all? 'Not the Bunny. Tailgate.' What in hell does that mean?"

"It's what he said. He didn't tell me what it meant."

"What's a tailgate got to do with anything?"

"I don't know that either."

"You don't know much, do you?" said Olive. "Well, well. Look at this, Dom. Our man here was a Fed." She turned and held out Sam's wallet and ID card. Agganis took them. I feigned a peek at them, but he frowned and waved me back.

"Come on," I said. "He died in my arms. Who was he? Who'd he work for?"

"I guess it won't be a secret for long," said Dom. "His name was Samuel Arbuckle, and he worked for the DIA. You ever heard of the DIA?"

"It's one of those alphabet agencies in Washington. I've read about it. What was a DIA agent doing on Martha's Vineyard?"

"Better yet, who killed him and why did he choose your yard to die in?"

"Yeah," said Olive, "how about that?"

"Maybe because he needed help and it was the first place he came to. Can I change out of these clothes now? I'm getting stickier by the minute."

Agganis nodded. "Okay, but put them in an evidence bag, and let me get some pictures of you first. Hey, Wilber, bring that camera over here."

Wilber took photos of me in my bloody clothes, and then more photos of my hands. He squinted at the hands.

"How come your hands aren't as bloody as the rest of you?"

"Because I washed them off before I called nine-one-one. I didn't want blood all over my phone."

"Oh, yeah?" He glanced at Agganis, shrugged, and walked off.

"You know what, Dom?" said Olive, still kneeling beside the body. "I think our man, here, got himself killed with a shotgun. He didn't know it was coming, either, because his own piece is still on his belt and his coat was zipped." She scowled at me. "Say, you probably have a shotgun. I think we'd better take a look at it. Maybe you blasted this guy yourself."

"You're in a sweet mood, as usual," I said to her. Then I turned to Dom. "Come on in with me and you can check out the gun cabinet while I clean up."

"I'll do that." He nodded at Olive. "Keep people away from the corpse and take a look in the guy's car."

I took a big evidence bag with me when we went inside. I use the outdoor shower seven months of the year, but by November I'm back indoors. While Dom poked through the gun cabinet I emptied my pockets, went into the bathroom, stripped, and put my bloody clothes in the bag. On the floor of the shower the water was pink for a while but finally cleared. I got into clean clothes and carried the evidence bag back out to the living room.

"Those long guns of yours are getting dusty," said Agganis. "How long has it been since you fired them?"

"Years. I keep them out of habit and in

case the kids want to be hunters when they grow up."

"I thought your wife had a small pistol along with this forty-five she shoots in competition. It's not here."

Dom had a long memory.

"She took it with her."

He studied me. "Why? She doesn't usually pack iron. You're not telling me everything. Why is Zee carrying? Why were you carrying just now? What's going on? You lied when you said you didn't know that guy, didn't you?"

I put up my swearing hand. "I never met him until he died in my arms. I'll take an oath on it."

"You ever talk to him? On the phone, maybe?"

"Not until he was dying. I told him I was going to call nine-one-one and he said those four words."

He shut the gun cabinet doors and locked them. "Where do you keep the key?"

"Put it up there on top, so I'll know where to find it."

"You're a burglar's best friend." He put his face close to mine. "Now stop this bullshit. You know more than you're telling me and I want it all. A man's been murdered. Worse yet, he's a Fed. This place will be swarming with his buddies within hours and they aren't going to be as nice to you as I am, so talk to me."

I had been considering the certain arrival of federal agents once Sam's death came to their attention. I figured that they'd be pressing me pretty hard to find out what I had to do with Sam, but I wasn't willing yet to put Joe Begay's name in the picture.

Instead, I said, "Okay, I'll tell you everything I know about that guy. It's not much." And I told him about Green Coat being in the Bunch of Grapes while I was there, then about seeing him across the street from the store, then about noticing the car following me and my effort to prevent the driver, who was Green Coat, from getting my license plate number.

"I think he got it anyway," I said in conclusion. "Anyway, the next time I saw him was here, today. When the car came into my yard I recognized it and got my pistol before I saw that I wouldn't need it."

"Why was he so interested in you?"

"I don't know."

"What made you think you might need a gun when you saw it was him? Cars have driven down here before and you never pulled a gun on any of their drivers."

"People don't usually follow me. I don't like it. Yesterday I moved my wife and kids out of here and over to John Skye's house till I can figure it out. That's why Zee has her Beretta."

"But you never knew who the guy was?"

"Not until just now."

"And you never talked to him?"

"Not until he was dying."

"And you never shot him?"

"You sound like Olive Otero. No, I never shot him, and I don't know who did. I don't even know for sure that he was shot, although he sure looked that way."

"You never heard a shot?"

I thought about that, then said, "I might have, but if I did I didn't think about it. This is deer season and you can hear guns go off sometimes."

"Yeah," said Dom. "There are hunters all over the place. If I wanted to walk up to somebody with a shotgun and not have them give it much thought, I'd put on an orange camouflage jacket and do it during hunting season."

I nodded. It has been said that the best time to murder somebody is on a battle-ground when bullets are flying everywhere. Hunting season is almost as good.

"You own an orange camouflage hunting jacket?" asked Dom.

"I have one in a closet somewhere. You want me to find it for you?"

He shook his head. "No. I have one, too, and so do about half the men on Martha's Vineyard. You sure you don't have any idea why Arbuckle came to die at your house?"

It was my turn to shake my head. "I think the chances are that my driveway was the first one he found and he knew he needed help. If it wasn't that, I'd say it was because he'd traced my plates and knew who I am and where I live, and that he came here on purpose, knowing that he was badly hurt and might not have much time to say what he had to say, and thinking that I was the best available person to get the message."

"Why would he think that?"

I didn't have to feign ignorance. "I have no idea. I don't know why he did it and I don't know the meaning of what he said. 'Not the Bunny. Tailgate.' Those are the words, but they mean nothing to me."

Dom rubbed his big hand on his big chin. "You know any Bunnies?"

"A long time ago I knew a girl called Bunny Montoya. And there are Playboy Bunnies, but I don't know any of them.

And there's the Easter Bunny." I heard the pause in my voice before I went on. "And there is or was a terrorist overseas who is or was called the Easter Bunny because he blew things up on religious holidays. I read about him somewhere. But Arbuckle didn't say it's the Bunny, he said it's not the Bunny."

"If it's not the Bunny," said Dom, "what is it? And what's a tailgate got to do with it?"

"Arbuckle was hurt badly. He may have been out of his mind."

"Did he sound like he was out of his mind?"

"No. His voice was faint but it sounded pretty sane as long as it lasted."

Agganis grunted. "Maybe the Feds can make something of it." He turned and went outside with me in his wake. Olive Otero was at the car. He walked over to her. "Anything interesting?"

"Look here," she said, pointing at the blood on the side of the car. "Looks like maybe it happened like this: Arbuckle gets out of the car and the perp blasts him immediately. He manages to get back into the car and drive away. He lived long enough to get here." She looked at me. "Unless Mr. Jackson killed him right here, that is."

"Maybe you know so much about what happened to Arbuckle because you did it yourself, Olive," I said. "Why don't you snap cuffs on yourself and run yourself in?"

"Why don't both of you just shut up?" said Dom. "Okay, boys, I guess we're about done here." He looked at a medic. "You can take the body away. Make sure it gets to the ME." Then he turned to me. "Now that you're all fresh and shiny, I'll need an official statement from you. You want to give it here or in my office?"

We did it in my living room with both of us talking into Olive Otero's tape recorder as he asked questions and I answered them. I left Joe Begay and Kate MacLeod out of my story, which shortened it a lot, but otherwise told the truth. Before I filled in the gaps I wanted to talk with Joe.

When he was done with his questions, Agganis rubbed his chin. "Any bright ideas about why the shooter didn't give Arbuckle a couple more rounds while he was at it? Finish him off right there?"

I shrugged. I'd wondered about that myself.

11

When the last police car had gone from my yard I wondered how long I could keep quiet about Joe and Kate.

One of the advantages of always telling all of the truth is that you never have to remember what you said. I was well past that point now, and not for the first time, since it's not unusual for me to keep some knowledge to myself. Usually it's just because some information doesn't seem important, but sometimes it's because revealing the whole truth might not be in my best interests or in the interests of someone I value. I try to avoid out-and-out lies, but when I do lie I rarely feel guilty about it. I would have lied about knowing where Anne Frank was hiding and not have lost a wink of sleep.

Most organizations, like most people, including me, tell mostly the truth most of the time. When the truth hurts, though, they ignore the issue, dance around it, tell half-truths and blatant lies, and attack their questioners to deflect attention from themselves. And there are certain organizations that will never tell you all of the truth unless they absolutely have to. Intelligence agencies, for instance. They hate bright lights.

I dislike and distrust secret organizations and official secret keepers. Tell me that a meeting or a decision or a policy is secret and I immediately suspect that the odor eaters are covering up a bad smell.

Still, right now I needed to know more about a couple of such agencies in particular and about U.S. intelligence operations in general. I knew that there were a lot of agencies and that the rivalries among them were legendary, but I needed to know more.

One of the two that interested me was Joe Begay's agency; but unfortunately for me Joe had never really told me where he worked, so I didn't know its name, if indeed it even existed. However, I did know who Samuel Arbuckle had worked for: the Defense Intelligence Agency, so I could start there.

All intelligence organizations being secretive by definition, I didn't expect to get a lot of information about the DIA. However, one never knows until one noses, so I drove to John Skye's house and sat down in front of our almost-brand-new computer. Zee was still at the hospital and the kids were at school, so I would have to do this on my own.

Fortunately for me, both Zee and the children were patient teachers, so even though I was a slow learner they had taught me how to take excursions into the Internet. I can't do complex things there, but I can do simple ones, so when Google gave me the opportunity to search for a subject, I typed in "Defense Intelligence Agency" and hit "enter."

And, lo! Up came a lot of information about the DIA, such as its origins, its organization, its purposes, its relationship to other government groups, and the assertion that it employed over seven thousand people. Seven thousand people!? No wonder my taxes were so high!

It didn't mention Samuel Arbuckle as one of the seven thousand, however, so I wasn't able to identify his role in the agency, and I wasn't surprised when I failed to find anything that suggested that the DIA was ever involved with anything illegal. Heaven forbid.

I thought about Sam. The fact that he had carried his ID with him suggested that he wasn't doing a chore that required him to deny his affiliation with his employer. That didn't tell me much, though.

Did the DIA operate both at home and abroad? If it did, would it say so?

I left the DIA's website and went back to Google. There I entered a search for "intelligence agencies."

Bonanza again! There was so much information about intelligence agencies that I could have spent the rest of my life reading it. I gave it a couple of hours.

First, I read newsmagazine and newspaper reports about general problems in the intelligence business: the separation between foreign and domestic intelligence and the relationships between the intelligence gatherers, the interpreters of that intelligence, and the policy makers who made decisions based upon those interpretations. I read about disagreements between agencies, about withheld information, about the consequences of good intelligence, bad intelligence, and improperly interpreted intelligence.

I read about which agencies specialized in particular kinds of intelligence and of their fondness for acronyms. I read about SIGINT, HUMINT, and OSINT and learned that the first referred to signals intelligence, such as cryptography, that the second was an acronym for intelligence gained from human sources, and that the last referred to so-called open intelligence, gained from sources such as newspapers, books, radio, and television. Right now I was apparently involved in a bit of OSINT of my own.

I thought of the ancient joke about government intelligence being an oxymoron.

I then went to official government websites and read that the United States intelligence community (known by the cognoscenti as "the CI") was currently defined by Executive Order 12333, and that it included dozens of separate agencies that employed tens of thousands of people, most of whom were doing pretty straightforward office work but some of whom were doing other, undescribed jobs.

I found and read Executive Order 12333. It was fourteen pages of small print and though most of it was mundane, some parts were more interesting. Paragraph 2.11, for example, prohibited IC personnel or others acting on behalf of the U.S. government from engaging in, or conspiring to engage in, assassination.

I wondered how the actions of Joe Begay's trade mission meshed with that directive. Not too well, at first glance, but maybe he and his associates had just helped some other anti-Bunny group to do the actual dirty work.

Paragraph 2.12, however, seemed to forbid any IC agency from participating or requesting any person to undertake activities forbidden by this order.

Hmmmm.

I came to paragraph 3.4(h), which defined "special activities." The definition of these was "activities conducted in support of national foreign policy objectives abroad which are planned and executed so that the role of the United States Government is not apparent or acknowledged publicly, and functions in support of such activities."

Hmmmm, again. An official provision that allowed the CI to do stuff they didn't want the public to know about. No surprise there, if you remembered CIA activities in Central and South America. And Joe's trade mission also fit the description of a special activity. Whenever official agencies don't want you to know what they do, you should probably get a clothespin for your nose.

The prohibition against assassination seemed to have been ignored more than once by the IC, and since Sam had died in my yard, I had a personal interest in violence involving the DIA.

I exited from Executive Order 12333 and after a couple of stumbles through the Web discovered a site that informed me that back in 2001, efforts had been made in Congress to eliminate the prohibition against assassinations. A House resolution that became known as the Terrorist Elimination Act would have legalized political assassinations by the CI. I couldn't find any confirmation that the resolution had passed, but I also couldn't find any that it hadn't.

Interestinger and interestinger. Zee's fears were apparently not wide of the mark. We were doing the same bad things the bad guys were doing to us. From some recess in my brain I drew a memory of an early American intelligence official who was even more naive than I was. He was said to have been furious when he discovered that efforts were being made to break another country's codes and to have exclaimed, "Gentlemen do not read other gentlemen's mail!" There were probably not too many gentlemen in the CI these days, and it was probably a good thing.

I was glad I'd gotten out of the Boston PD when I did. Peacekeeping was a rough business and seemed to be getting rougher.

The Homeland Security Act came to mind, so I checked that out. The document was so long that I wondered if anyone had actually read it all. Certainly I didn't. I did note a few things, however. The paragraph headed "Construction: Severability" seemed to say that if any provision of the act should be held to be invalid or unenforceable, it should nevertheless be construed so as to give it maximum effect permitted by law, unless it was utterly invalid or unenforceable, in which case it should be omitted from the act.

Either this concept was murky or my brain was. Maybe both. I skimmed on down through pages of governmentese before giving up and calling it quits. Someone once said that one requirement of research was a love of drudgery. My talent in the field was obviously thin.

One thing was clear, though: the Homeland Security Department was a gigantic bureaucracy at least the equal in size and power of the incredibly huge CI. No wonder people who perceived themselves as humanists and defenders of civil liberties and open government were getting nervous. But then, such people have always been nervous Nellies, according to their critics.

Come back, Cassandra! I'll believe you this time in spite of the gods!

But neither Cassandra nor Maat appeared, so I got off the Net and phoned Joe Begay.

12

"Something's happened that might interest you," I said when he answered his cell phone. "I'm coming over."

I hung up before he could say no, got into the Land Cruiser, and drove to Aquinnah. Two trips in one day. I seemed to be spending a lot of time there lately. The woods were mostly bare-branched trees, and the few leaves that remained on them and covered the ground beneath them were the color of metal: gold, copper, bronze, and rusted iron. The sky looked cold.

No one seemed to be following me but, just in case I was wrong, when I got to Aquinnah I took Lobsterville Road, then cut right onto Lighthouse Road and pulled over to the side. Nobody came around the corner behind me, so I went on to Uncle Bill's house.

Uncle Bill's old Ford was in the yard, but Kate's rental car was not. Whither Kate? I wondered.

I knocked on the door. No one opened it. I knocked louder, and allowed myself the beginning of a worry.

"Don't beat the door down," said Joe's voice from behind me. "It's not locked."

I turned and saw him coming out of the woods from the direction of his own house, which was about a half mile away at the northern edge of the clay cliffs that had given Gay Head its name. He was wearing camouflage hunting clothes and carrying a shotgun. The best possible cover during hunting season.

He poked a thumb over his shoulder. "I got your call while I was in the woods. Come on inside." He glanced at the two vehicles in the yard, frowned briefly, and led me into the house. "You see Kate?" he asked.

"No. Not since this morning, here with you."

"She said she was going to stay here."

"Women don't always do what they say."

"Neither do men." He put his shotgun in a closet. "You cut off your call pretty fast."

"I didn't want to spend much time on the line."

He arched a brow. "You think some-body's tapping your phone?"

"I don't know, but I wouldn't be sur-prised if somebody was trying to trace you through yours. I don't know how they do it, but I know it can be done."

He nodded. "It can be done, but nobody has bugged this room yet, so tell me about this something that brings you up here into Indian country."

I told him about Samuel Arbuckle's de-mise in my driveway and my conversations with Dom Agganis. "I didn't mention you or Kate," I said, "because I wanted you to know about what happened first."

He looked thoughtful. "Dom is going to be pretty pissed off when he finds out."

"Maybe he won't find out."

"Oh, he'll find out, all right. He's bound to have called Washington about Arbuckle, and DIA agents are probably already on their way. One of their own is dead and they'll want to talk with you about it and with Dom, too. There'll be a lot of narrow eyes and sniffing noses, and it'll be hard to keep anything from them."

"I'll tell them what I told Dom. No more, no less. The only other people who know about Arbuckle following Kate are you and her. If either of you decides to talk about that, I'll suddenly remember it, too. What are they going to do? Throw me in jail?"

"That's exactly what they'll try to do. Obstruction of justice, lying to the police, Homeland Security, and all like that."

It wasn't a pleasant prospect. "Did you know Samuel Arbuckle?" I asked.

He shook his head. "I don't know the name. You sure of those last words of his?"

"I'm sure. Did you ever hear Kate mention Arbuckle?"

"No, but it's no secret that she has an active social life with a lot of men in it."

"But she said she didn't recognize him when she was in Vineyard Haven."

"She also said she really didn't get a good look at him."

"Yeah, but I can't imagine her not recognizing him if he was a boyfriend. Do you suppose she might have been lying?"

"It's possible. What do you think?"

"I thought she was being straight, but I'm not hard to fool."

Begay went to the stove and tapped a finger on the coffeemaker. "Still warm. She hasn't been gone long. Kate is a beautiful woman and she lives in a town where a lot of people know each other."

There was something elusive about him.

"Arbuckle was married," I said. "I saw a photo in his wallet. He had a pretty wife and two kids."

"A lot of married guys chase the girls, so that means nothing." Joe got two cups from a cabinet. "What means something is what he said to you: 'Not the Bunny. Tailgate.' He had to be talking about the Easter Bunny. Anything else would be too coincidental. What was he trying to tell you? That it wasn't the Bunny who shot him? And what's that got to do with a tailgate?"

"That it wasn't the Bunny, whatever that means. Is Tailgate a code name or the name of a place? A bar, maybe? He thought the name was important because he used his last breath to say so."

Joe poured coffee and handed me a cup. "I never heard of Tailgate. Why did he come to your house to die? Why you?"

It was a popular question and I gave him the answer I'd given Dom Agganis: that it was either coincidental or because he knew who I was and decided to trust me.

"Why would he trust you, of all people?"

"I told Dom I didn't know, and I don't. But if I was to guess, I'd say that Arbuckle probably checked me out after he got my license plate. If he did, he knew where I

136

lived and he knew I wasn't in the spook business and that I was basically pretty uninteresting except for the fact that I seemed to know Kate. If he was watching when I checked for a tail on her car as she drove out of town, he might have decided that I was a friend of hers and maybe even knew something about her work. Maybe that made me trustworthy in his mind. When he got shot, he didn't have much time to decide what to do, so he may have just taken the best chance he had."

"Any idea why he was following Kate?"

"You tell me. You're in the spook business."

He let that go by without comment, and again I sensed elusiveness in him. He sipped his coffee and looked out the window.

"If Kate was here, maybe she could tell us," he said at last. Then he allowed himself a quick bit of temper. "Where the hell is she?" As quickly as it had come, the anger was gone. "If it isn't the Bunny, who is it?"

I had been thinking about that, but not too clearly. "Did the three other people on the trade mission, the three dead ones, have enemies other than the Easter Bunny?"

Joe's expression didn't change. "Everybody has enemies."

"I mean enemies mad enough to kill them."

"There are probably people abroad who didn't shed any tears when they learned they were dead."

"Who knew about the membership of the trade mission?"

Joe shook his head. "You won't get any names from me, but you can guess that a lot of thought and planning went into the job and that a good many people were involved. All of them knew something about it. The Boss and his top people knew everything."

"How about his secretary?"

"He'd know. And so would a few other people with top clearance. Not too many, though, because they'd want to maintain plausible deniability in case something went wrong."

"You mean that if things got screwed up, you five mission people were on your own?"

"That's how it works. State would try to help us out because we're American citizens, but they wouldn't necessarily know why we were over there."

"None of you had official government jobs that could be traced?"

He stared at me, then shrugged. "I'm in

the private sector. I haven't worked for the government since I retired from the army twenty years ago."

"But the trade mission, at least the part having to do with the Easter Bunny and his friends, had to be a government job. You worked for a guy you call the Boss. You did contract work for Washington."

"I don't remember ever saying that, and I don't think anyone will find any paperwork that says it. You'll be better off leaving this alone."

"So I'll have deniability, too?"

"Something like that. The less you know about this sort of thing the less dangerous you are to certain people. It's not a good thing to have those people thinking about you."

I felt my hands forming fists. "You must mean some people here in America. No foreign terrorist would mind if I spilled the beans about any of this business. Are you telling me that there are American agents willing to assassinate other Americans who might know things they shouldn't know?"

His wide face revealed no emotion. "If there are such people, I don't know of them, and I think I'd have heard. I know there are conspiracy buffs who believe there are secret government assassination groups working out of Washington, but I've never heard of any policy authorizing such activities. It's possible that some rogue agent might do something like that on his own, but if he did he'd be treated like any other murderer. Still, it's better if you're not inside the circle of people who interests the authorities."

That was probably true. Even in small towns it's better not to be "known to the police," as most local perps are. Once you're known, you get watched. I willed my fists back into hands.

"What I'm wondering," I said, "is whether somebody besides the Bunny may be in action here, and what that person or those people are up to."

Joe's stony lips flickered through a brief smile. "I've wondered about that myself, and so have some other people, in Washington. You don't look surprised."

"I'm not," I said. "I haven't had very many original ideas during my life. Most of my best ones turn out to have been written down by some Greek or Roman several thousand years ago. What does Kate think?"

His smile was gone. "We could ask her if she was here."

But Kate wasn't there, and we didn't know where she was or why.

13

"I don't know much about Kate," I said. "What do you know?"

I thought his stony face became even stonier, but all he said was "Enough to trust her on jobs. She did good work during the trade mission."

"Had you worked with her before?"

"Once. On an earlier job. She was good that time, too. Very professional."

"You say she has an active social life. What do you know about that?"

He eyed me carefully over his coffee cup. "I've heard the scuttlebutt about her being a popular girl at home, and I believe it, but she never let her private life interfere when she was working with me. I don't investigate people's personal lives unless it's part of an assignment."

That last sentence interested me. "One of the jobs you do is checking out people's private lives? I thought the FBI usually did that."

"Other outfits do it, too." His lips formed a cold smile. "There are a lot of rivalries among agencies. They don't always trust one another to give them the true scoop on something."

"Would the DIA be interested in checking out Kate?"

He glanced out the window. "Maybe."

Why the glance? "Why would they be interested?"

His eyes came back and his smile faded. "I'll ask them when they come to see me. It shouldn't be too long before they're here."

"Does Kate have a shotgun to go along with that pistol of hers?"

He studied me. "You think she may have blasted Arbuckle?"

"It's a thought."

He shook his head. "In the first place, I don't think she has a shotgun. In the second, if she and Arbuckle were enemies he wouldn't have let her get close to him with a shotgun. And if they were friends she wouldn't have any reason to shoot him."

"Unless he thought they were friends and she thought otherwise."

"You're getting cynical in your old age, J.W. Where would she have gotten the gun?"

"Maybe she stole it. Half the houses on Martha's Vineyard have shotguns in them. With her training I imagine she could have gotten into some place without any trouble at all."

"She could manage that, but I still don't make her for the shooter. She'd have had to steal the gun, then arrange to meet Arbuckle someplace private, then show up with the gun, and shoot him before he knew what was happening. And she'd have had to do all that very quickly. What time did Arbuckle come down your road?"

I told him. "It wasn't long after I got home from seeing you and Kate earlier today. I see what you mean about *quickly*. She was here with you when I left."

He nodded. "And she was still here when I left about fifteen minutes later to scout my house. Doesn't leave her much time to kill Arbuckle."

"Unless she already had the gun and a date to meet him."

"It would still be tight."

"Maybe too tight. But she went somewhere."

His mouth suggested annoyance. "Yeah,

143

she went somewhere. I'll be glad when this is over and she's back home in Bethesda."

I thought of Joe and Kate together here in this old house. He was an attractive man and she was an attractive woman. Five days was a long time, and Toni Begay was far away.

"Has she mentioned knowing any other men here?" I asked. "Say, a Washington suit with a house on the Vineyard? There are a lot of D.C. people with places here."

He nodded. "If she knows anybody here, she hasn't mentioned his name."

"Can you find out?"

Another nod. "I can ask her when I see her. Meanwhile, I can make some calls. Someone should know."

"While you're calling, can you find out why the DIA is interested in her? Why was Arbuckle watching her?"

"I can try. Right now, though, we should decide what to tell the DIA people who'll be investigating his death. I think the best thing for you to do is fess up and tell them everything you know. That should get you off the hook."

"What about you and Kate? If I talk, they'll know about both of you and about the Easter Bunny, too."

"A lot of people know about the Easter

Bunny, and I can handle the DIA."

I sat for a moment and ran things through my mind. Then I looked at Joe and said, "Tell me something, Sarge, was the DIA involved in the trade mission?"

He said nothing.

"It occurs to me," I said, "that maybe the hit on Rudolph and Scarecrow and the Bunny was a DIA caper, and that your boss contracted to do the job for them. Is that what happened?"

"I wouldn't know."

But I thought he did know. "Because if that's the scenario, it explains a lot of things: the DIA knows all about the Bunny probably doing Susan in, at least, and now trying to do in you and Kate, too. That would explain why Arbuckle was here: he wasn't after Kate; he was trying to make sure the Bunny didn't get to her. She didn't know who he was, but he knew who she was. He was probably hoping to nail the Bunny, but apparently the Bunny nailed him first." I looked at him. "What do you think of that scenario?"

"No comment."

I noticed that my right forefinger was tapping the table all on its own, as if it had its own little metronome in its own little brain. "If I'm right," I said, "maybe we should leave the Bunny to the DIA guys. There'll soon be a lot more of them here than there are of him."

"You have a lot of confidence in government agencies," said Joe.

"Tell me something else," I said. "Does Kate date guys who work for the DIA?"

"I don't know who Kate dates."

"With all the IC snoops in Washington watching each other, somebody must know."

"Not necessarily. There were guys at the FBI who were spying for the other side for years before they finally got caught. Looking back, it's pretty clear that somebody should have noticed them, but nobody did."

True. Two popular unanswerable questions are "Why didn't you see that?" and "Why didn't you think of that?" I've never known why I never thought of or noticed things that later seemed to have been perfectly obvious.

"It's something else to ask her when I see her," said Begay. "But why do you want to know?"

I wasn't sure. "It's just that with her being in the spook business, I thought she might naturally gravitate to other spooks. The way cops have bars where they can hang out with other cops and not have to worry about being misunderstood by civilians."

Begay shook his head. "Most people in the IC are just normal people who work in an office and go home to their families at night. Their friends aren't necessarily people in the business."

I stood up. "I don't suppose you'll change your mind and tell me if I'm right about the DIA being behind the hit on the Bunny bunch."

"No, I don't suppose I will." He paused, then said, "But I don't know if you should reject the idea."

That was as much as I was going to get from Joe.

"Any sign of enemy activity down at your house?" I asked.

"None. But I'm a patient man. He has to come sooner or later."

"Maybe he fell for your car-at-the-airport trick. Maybe he thinks you're really gone."

"Those 'he knows that I know that he knows that I know that he knows' games can go on forever, but I think the Bunny will bite my bait. Especially if he knows Kate is on the island."

"How would he know that?"

"My guess would be that somebody told him."

"Who?"

"I don't know. Yet."

I stood up. "Be careful, Joe."

"Yes. You go home and try to stay out of this if you can."

"I will," I said, but I thought it was too late for that.

I drove home on the gray road between the barren trees and past the steely water. It was a chilly day, with a north wind making it even colder. The gray clouds looked heavy and there was a feeling of snow in the air. The hunters would be wearing their down vests and wool shirts under their camouflage jackets. They'd like a little snow to muffle their steps and to show them the tracks of the deer. As if on demand, a few flakes began to blow across the road. They soon became thicker, and by the time I passed the airport I had to turn on my windshield wipers.

I wondered if the Bunny, thinking ahead, had brought his own winter hunting duds and shotgun to the island and whether he had bought his out-of-state hunting license so as to be legal and in the clear if some warden stopped him.

From time to time I checked my rearview mirror, but saw no one following me through the blowing snow. At the end of our driveway I stopped and picked up our mail from the mailbox. If anyone wanted to find me, all he had to do was look at the name on the box.

Perhaps that accounted for the car tracks leading into our driveway but not leading out again. A visitor had arrived since the snow had begun to fall and was still here.

I felt a chill that had nothing to do with the weather.

14

I drove a few yards down the driveway and parked between two large oak trees that grew close to the track. The trees and the battered old Land Cruiser made an excellent roadblock. No one would be driving away from the house unless I wanted them to.

I got out and walked directly into the woods. There I put my car keys on the top of a low branch of one of the big oak trees, on the off chance that my visitor might have occasion to search me and then use the keys to move the truck. I wanted his car to stay in my yard even if he managed to get the drop on me.

The chances were that the driver was a neighbor, or maybe even Zee herself.

But maybe not. The old comic definition of paranoia came to mind: two noia.

I went through the oak brush and between leafless trees, circling down toward the house. The snow flurries offered all the camouflage I'd have, but I'd be approaching from the back of my shed so my visitor would have to be looking in the right direction if he was to see me before I got a first look at him.

Beneath my feet the crackle of dry leaves was muffled by the snow, and I wished it was later in the day, when there would be less light. I also wished I had my old .38 that Olive Otero had been so quick to take into her possession.

Mr. Wishful.

I saw the house and shed ahead of me through the trees, darker shapes in the falling white snow. Then, beyond the corner of the house, I made out the rear end of a dark car parked in the yard. Was the driver in the car or somewhere else?

I circled farther out, then came back, keeping the shed between me and the house. The clasp that held the shed door shut was still closed, meaning that no one was inside. I peeked around the corner of the shed at the house and saw no signs of footprints in the snow by the back door or the movement of curtains in the rear windows.

I waited and listened and then trotted to

the back door and looked through its window into the kitchen. No one was there. I don't lock my doors, so I was inside in only a moment. I walked to the door of the living room, avoiding the squeaky part of the floor and listening all the way.

No sound. I peeked through the door. Empty.

Making no sound myself, I moved through the rooms in the house. There aren't many and no one was in any of them. Oliver Underfoot and Velcro yawned hello from the guest room bed, and decided not to get up and join me. They seemed unconcerned with any visitor.

I saw no sign of melting snow on the living room floor. Was it possible that my visitor actually took closed doors seriously and hadn't tried the front doorknob?

I heard the car's motor start and looked out the front window. The car was Kate's and she was turning it around.

What was she doing here?

I went out through the screened porch and waved to her. She looked surprised and then smiled, stopped the car, and got out.

"Where did you come from?" she asked, walking toward me. "I knocked, but no one answered. Then I waited, but no one came down the driveway. And now, just as I was leaving, here you are."

"I went for a walk," I said.

"Are you going to invite me in? In case you didn't notice, it's snowing."

"Sure," I said. She smiled up at me as she passed, and I sensed a siren in my presence and understood why Odysseus had himself lashed to the mast. I followed her into the house.

The first thing that caught her eye was the framed gun magazine cover on the wall that pictured Zee at one of her early pistol competitions. She hadn't won that one but her looks had made her a cover girl anyway.

"Your wife?" asked Kate.

"Yes."

"She's very beautiful."

"Yes. And a crack shot, too."

Kate looked around. "How cozy. I like the way you have your fishing poles hanging across the ceiling."

"On Martha's Vineyard, we call them rods, not poles," I said, going to the stove and sticking in a couple more pieces of wood. "We keep them in here because this is the only room big enough to hold them."

"I don't suppose you have some coffee."

"It won't take long to make some."

"I'd love a cup. Do you mind if I walk around and look at things?"

"Not at all. Take off your coat." I took off my own, then made coffee and carried two cups back into the living room.

She came out of the guest room and took one of the cups. She was wearing slacks and a loose winter sweater that hid her pistol but did little to disguise her body. Her eyes were warm.

"I love your house."

"It's an old hunting camp my father bought a long time ago when land on the island was still cheap."

"It's exactly the kind of house I imagined you'd have."

She sat at one end of the couch and looked down at the locks and lockpicks I kept on the coffee table. "My, are you a locksmith, too?"

"I got the picks at a yard sale from a woman who didn't know what they were. I practice picking when I'm in the mood."

I sat down in Archie Bunker's chair. Every house has an Archie Bunker's chair. Mine was, like all of them, old and comfortable. I'd gotten it from the town dump in the golden years before the environmentalists changed dumps into landfills where you could no longer shop for good, free, used stuff you needed.

"Isn't lock-picking illegal?" Her tone suggested that she didn't care if it was.

"I don't think it's illegal to pick your own," I said.

"Are those the only ones you pick?" Her smile curled up the corners of her mouth and her eyes were dancing and hungry.

Out of some dusty mental cranny came the words of a nearly forgotten Elizabethan ballad:

> *Poor kit hath lost her key,*
> *But I have one to fit*
> *Her lock if she will try*
> *And do me not deny;*
> *I hope she hath more wit.*

"What brings you here, Kate?" I asked.

She wound a lock of her hair around a finger. "I'm nervous. I'm not getting much comfort from Joe. He wants me to stay in that house and do nothing while he goes out and takes care of the Easter Bunny. I've been away from home for a long time.

I need distraction." She looked at me with her hot eyes. "I need a man."

I felt a little of that heat inside myself. "It's not safe for you to be distracted," I said. "There's a killer on the island and he seems to be after you."

"I don't have a choice. I'm one of those women who need a man every now and then. I don't want one for a husband or a longtime relationship, at least not yet. I just need one for right now."

"I'm afraid I can't help you."

"It's been weeks. Since before the Bunny spiked Susan Bancroft's scotch then shot her full of enough dope to kill an elephant." She paused, then said almost dreamily, "The Bunny just missed getting me at the same time, you know. If he'd come a day earlier, he would have."

My ears went up. "You were with Susan the day before she died?"

"Why not? We were friends and her boyfriend was out of town. Your wife isn't here today. Come and sit beside me. It'll be good for us both. And don't worry, because your wife will never know; I don't break up marriages." She patted the couch with one hand and touched her tongue to her lips.

"I'm tempted but taken," I said, showing her my wedding ring to emphasize the point.

"I won't take you anywhere you don't want to go." She started to rise but something in my face stopped her. "Don't be so damned righteous. And for God's sake, take that look of sympathy off your face!" She sank down again. "What is it about you damned islanders? First Joe and now you!"

"There are plenty of island men who'll bed you in a second," I said. "And I wouldn't blame them. Ten years ago I'd have been first in line."

She picked up her coffee cup and drank. "Sure. But not now. Jesus, I'm going crazy. You have no idea!"

But she was wrong about that; though I had read the Fire Sermon, I had never achieved the cessation of desire.

"Before you start manhunting," I said, "I want you to tell me something. It's important."

"I've already told you what's important to me and you've dusted me off."

"My wife is all the woman I want or can handle," I said. "Do you know a man named Samuel Arbuckle?"

She looked surprised. "I know the name.

I met him once, in fact. He's a friend of a friend. Why?"

"Was he one of your lovers?"

Her lips tightened. "I don't talk about my lovers. They're no one's business but mine."

"I don't think he was, because you'd have recognized him in Vineyard Haven when you saw him. But it will help if I know for sure."

She studied me. "The answer is no. Are you telling me that was Sam Arbuckle who followed me out of the bookstore?"

"Yes. And who followed me later. What do you know about him?"

She thought for a moment. "Not much. He works out of the Pentagon. A guy I was seeing talked about him sometimes. The two of them had been on some project together, I think. I remember that Arbuckle and his wife came by our booth one time when Stephen and I were having dinner. Arbuckle is a good-looking guy. We all had one of those little tableside chats before they went on their way. Why? Is he here because of me?"

She had an eye for men, all right. She'd met him once and remembered his looks. "He's not watching you any longer," I said. "He's dead."

"What?" Her eyes widened.

I gestured toward the yard where her car was parked. "Somebody shotgunned him this morning, but he was tough and drove here before he died. Does the word *tailgate* mean anything to you?"

15

Her coffee cup was still in her hand. She carefully put it down on the table. "What are you talking about? As far as I know, when you tailgate somebody, it means you're driving too close behind."

"You don't know of a place by that name, or maybe a project with that code name?"

"No. Why do you ask?"

I told her about what had happened that morning, and repeated Arbuckle's last words. "What do you think he meant?" I asked. "Was his bunny our Bunny? And what did he mean by tailgate?"

She was impatient. "Of course he was talking about the Easter Bunny! There aren't any other bunnies in the picture!" Then she seemed to slow her thoughts. "Tailgate? I can't imagine what that means, but if it's not the Easter Bunny, maybe

Arbuckle was telling you that we're wrong in thinking that it was." She looked at me. "Maybe it's someone else who's doing the killing."

And when she said that, I no longer saw through a glass, darkly. "He didn't say 'tailgate,'" said my voice. "He said, 'Tell Kate,' but he was on his last breath and I heard him wrong. He said, 'Tell Kate.'" I looked at her, full of certainty. "And now he has told you, and you've understood. It's not the Easter Bunny; it's someone else who's doing the killing."

Her brow furrowed, and my own thoughts raced through the many reasons people have for killing other people.

Some of those reasons are so whimsical as to be incomprehensible: people kill just to see what it feels like; they kill to experience power or joy or sorrow or some other emotion that life doesn't otherwise provide. They kill because God or Satan tells them to, or to save the world from aliens from outer space; they kill out of patriotic or religious or tribal fervor.

But mostly they kill for simple motives such as greed, fear, sex or its lack, and revenge. They kill to get what someone else has, to defend themselves, to get love or destroy the lover who's left them, or to get even.

Books have been written about why people kill. One thing they agree about is that every murder involves several stories: the story of the killer, the story of the victim, the story of the two participants coming fatally together through time and space, and, if efforts are made to solve the crime, the story of the detective.

"How many lovers have you had?" I asked Kate. "How many men? How many women?"

Her dark eyes flashed. "I told you to leave my lovers out of this conversation. My private life is my own business!"

I put up a hand. "I personally don't care if you sleep with baboons three times a day, but whoever killed Arbuckle and Susan Bancroft has a history that links him with them and with you and Joe Begay. The list of such people can't be too long, but it might include your boyfriends past and present. How many are there?"

She lifted her chin and her voice was defiant. "A thousand!"

That was a different man every week for more than twenty years. She annoyed me. "We don't have time for lies. How many?"

She tossed her long, dark hair. "I'm thirty-five. I had my first boy when I was fourteen and my first schoolteacher a month later. I've been sexually active all my life."

"No husbands along the way?"

"None of my own. I've had offers but I wasn't interested."

"Maybe it's just as well."

Anger only made her more attractive, and I could see why she could have almost any man she wanted.

Then she surprised me by saying, "I'm about ready to give up this kind of life and to get married. And when I do, I'm going to be monogamous. There'll be no more lovers in hotel rooms. We'll have a house and a family and we'll live normal lives."

She must have seen something in my face as I listened, because she pushed her hair back with both hands and smiled an ironic smile. "Yes, yes. I know that you're thinking about me and Joe and about me and you. All I can say is that I'm not married yet."

"Not counting Joe and me," I said, "how many men and women have you had?"

"I'm not interested in bedding women."

"Stop dancing. How many men, then?"

"I don't notch a tally stick."

"Narrow it down. How many were un-happy when you left them?"

She smiled her shining smile. "All of them, I hope."

Earlier she had resented my intrusion into her private life, but now she seemed to be almost enjoying it.

"How many of them were really angry?"

She arched a brow. "Not many. All of them knew it was just one of those things."

"But some weren't satisfied with a trip to the moon on gossamer wings?"

"A few. I eased their feelings when I could, and broke the relationships off when they wouldn't be eased." A small frown appeared on her face. "Are you thinking that some lover of mine is doing all this killing? I don't think so."

"You're in the spook business and you must know people who know how to kill people."

The frown remained. "I don't know any who would want to do something like this!"

"Don't look back too far. Just, say, the past four or five years. Anyone there who didn't want it to be just one of those fabulous flights?"

"I can't think of any."

"How about the people who worked with you? How about Edo and Francis and Susan, for instance? Did you bed them?"

Her anger returned, but its flame was lower than before. "I told you, I don't have sex with women. What if I did sleep with Edo and Francis? All three of them are dead, so none of them is doing this!"

"Do you make a habit of sleeping with all of the men you work with? Wasn't one of the reasons you came here so you could make a play for Joe Begay?"

She gave a wry smile. "And I struck out. It doesn't happen often."

I imagined it didn't. "Joe says that one reason he trusts you is because he worked with you earlier and you can be depended on to do your job. Who worked on that earlier mission?"

She thought for a moment. "Susan and Joe and Stephen."

"The same Susan?"

"Yes. Susan Bancroft. In my business you work with the same people sometimes."

"You told me that you and Susan weren't lovers. What about Stephen?"

She made a small sweeping gesture with one hand. "As far as I was concerned, it was over between Stephen and me before that assignment. He made a play for Susan, but she had a boyfriend at home and she said no in pretty strong words."

Kate smiled a humorless smile. "Susan and I were different people, as you can tell. Anyway, Stephen was furious with Susan, and then he got badly hurt as we were coming out. We got him home and they patched him up as well as they could." She shook her head and the light danced on her long, dark hair. "I don't think he's your man, unless your killer uses a wheelchair."

"Does he have a last name?"

"Harkness. Stephen was our communications guy. He may still be in the IC, sitting at a desk somewhere, but I don't think he's up to fieldwork anymore."

"Anyone else I should check on?"

"Old lovers or just anyone at all?"

Her tone was almost gentle and I was aware that I had been alternating between liking her and not liking her. There had been no alteration in my body's awareness of her beauty and sensuality.

I said, "Anyone at all who has a tie with the trade mission and who might want the members all dead. Other than the Easter Bunny, that is."

"I thought we'd eliminated the Easter Bunny."

I shook my head. "Arbuckle might have, but I haven't eliminated anyone. I'm trying to add to the list before I start subtracting.

Can you think of anyone who might have wanted the trade mission crew dead?"

"No."

"I'll settle for the names of other pissed-off lovers and of people who had ties to the mission."

"It won't be much of a list, because I don't know who planned the mission or knew about it, other than some foreign assets who helped us out over there. And I think you can discount them because most of them were local and were glad to help ax Rudolph and the Scarecrow."

"Any of them make it to your bed?"

She smiled and shook her head. "I had no time for foreign affairs, if you'll pardon the expression. Worse luck, too. One of the boys was a good-looking lad."

"Americans, then. Anybody who went away mad sometime in the last five years."

"It'll be a short list."

I gave her pen and paper. "Write down addresses and anything else you can remember."

She hesitated. "What are you going to do with this? Some of these guys are married with kids. I don't want to wreck any innocent lives."

"They don't sound too innocent to me."

She shook her head. "What a puritan

you are. They're men who like sex, that's all. Hell, so do you and I. We're not talking immorality here." But she bent over the paper and wrote one name and then others.

When she was done, she handed the paper to me. "Here. These men didn't want to break off with me, but none of them is a killer."

"We'll see."

"I know a killer when I meet one."

"Do you sleep with them anyway?"

She stood and came close to me. "A couple, maybe. How about you? How about changing your mind?" She leaned over me and her arms went around my neck.

I could feel the magnetic heat of her body pulling me to her.

Maybe I hesitated, but then I put my hands on her arms and pushed them away.

"No."

"You want to."

"I don't always do what I want to do."

"Why not?"

"Not because I'm moral. Probably because I'm not but think I should be."

She eyed me, then shook her head. "You and Joe Begay are two of a kind."

"I call that flattery."

She smiled a beautiful crooked smile. "I call it a mystery. Two guys like you on one little island. I guess I'll have to start hitting the bars if I want any action."

"You won't have any trouble finding what you're looking for there, but be careful. There's a killer around and we don't know who it is. But he knows you."

Her hand strayed to and then from her hip, where her pistol was holstered. "Don't worry about me. What are you going to do with that list of names? I don't want anybody to get into trouble because of me."

"They're already in trouble because of you," I said. "My truck's blocking the driveway. I'll bring it down and then you can be on your way."

16

It had been a long day, but I still had a stop to make before I headed to my family at John Skye's farm. It was confession time. I got into the truck and drove to the state police barracks in Oak Bluffs.

Dom's office was on Temahigan Road in a building that for years had been painted an unstylish blue but had then been refinished with cedar shingles, which were now properly weathered and much more Vineyardy.

When I pulled off the road and stopped in the narrow parking space in front of the building, I took note of two other cars already in the back parking lot. They had that rental look about them, an impression confirmed when I saw local stickers in their windows. First Kate, then Arbuckle, and now these two drivers were contributing to the island's winter economy.

Crime was paying for local car renters.

I went inside and found four men with Dom in his office. Their stylish winter coats were open, showing suits and ties beneath. On Martha's Vineyard, only lawyers and Mormon missionaries wear suits and ties, but these guys weren't islanders. Their voices stopped when I appeared and they looked at me with flat eyes.

"Well, well," said Dom, looking over his desk. "We were just talking about you, J.W."

One of the men hooked a thumb at me and asked, "Is this him? Is this Jackson?"

"This is him," said Dom. "We were about to go looking for you, J.W., but you've saved us the effort. These gentlemen want to hear your version of what happened to their colleague Samuel Arbuckle."

"That's right," said another of the men. "We want your story."

DIA people for sure. "I need to talk to you," I said to Dom.

"These gentlemen represent the United States government," said Dom, "and they need to talk to you. You can talk with me afterward."

"I'd like to talk with you first," I said. "It won't take long."

The tallest of the four men showed his ID card. "We're from the Defense Intelligence Agency," he said. "We'd appreciate hearing anything you can tell us about Agent Arbuckle."

His eyes were on the level with mine. I looked into them. "I want to talk with Sergeant Agganis first," I said, "then I'll tell you everything I know."

"I think we have priority here," said the man. "A man's been murdered."

I looked past him. "Dom, I want a minute of your time."

"I don't think you understand," said the tall man. "We have a special interest in this case and every minute is important." His voice was touched with temper and he put a hand on my arm.

I looked at the hand, and as I did I heard Dom's voice: "All right, J.W. Let's all relax, gentlemen. J.W., let's step down the hall."

The hand hesitated then left my arm and I looked into its owner's eyes. Dom rounded his desk and waved toward a door. He and I went through the door and into a small room off the hall.

"Those guys are already mad," he said. "Don't make things worse. Now what is it that's so damned important that it can't wait?"

"I've had a memory improvement. There are some things you should know."

His eyes narrowed. "Like what? Your ass can be in a sling if you've been lying to me. Talk. You've got one minute!"

"It'll take more time than that," I said, and I told him the whole story. When I was done, I said, "I don't know what's going on, but I know it's something you should know about. I'm sorry I didn't tell you sooner, but —"

"But you didn't want our sights to land on your friend Begay," snapped Agganis. "Very loyal of you, I'm sure, but not very bright!"

"I think the local police should be told," I said. "There's a killer wandering around loose and —"

"I think I know who to talk to!" said Dom. "Jesus, Olive may be right about you belonging in jail."

"I said I was sorry. You want to hear it again?"

"No! What I want is more cooperation than I've gotten so far. You can start by telling those suits out there what you've just told me."

"I don't want to get Joe Begay in trouble."

"Joe Begay is already in trouble. We're

trying to get him out of it. Come on."

We walked back to his office and into the stares of four pairs of eyes. "J.W. has a story to tell you," said Dom in a calm voice, sitting down behind his desk. "When he's through you can ask him any questions you want."

I started with Joe Begay coming into my shed while I was scalloping and went from then to now, leaving out nothing but some of my wilder conjectures.

When I was through, one of the men said, "So this woman, this Kate MacLeod, put the moves on you, eh?"

I shrugged. "She likes men. It was nothing personal."

"And she's also hot for this Joe Begay, this friend of yours who told you he was on this trade mission?"

"That's my impression."

"And you think maybe it's one of her ex-beaus who's knocking off her new loves?"

"It seems possible."

"And this guy shot Arbuckle?"

I don't know if you can hear a curled lip, but I thought I detected one around his voice. "I don't know who shot Arbuckle or why," I said. "All I know is what I've told you."

"The woman told you she knew Arbuckle?"

"She said she'd met him briefly in a restaurant while she was dining with a friend who knew him."

"We'll check out Arbuckle, the woman, and Begay, and those names she gave you," said the tall man. "Where can we find MacLeod and Begay?"

Dom and I exchanged glances. "You won't find Joe unless he wants you to," I said. "I'll give you his cell phone number. You can talk with him and arrange a meeting."

"You know where he is," said the fourth man, who up to now had said nothing. "If we phone him, he'll have time to split. Tell us where he is."

I looked at him. "I know Joe and I trust him. I don't know you four from a pile of shit. He won't run away, but I don't know where he is, so don't ask. Call him. That's what I do when I want to see him." I gave him Begay's cell phone number.

"We can triangulate his phone and find him," said another of the men. "Sergeant Agganis, I suggest that you put your friend here in jail and keep him there until this is over. If he's got a cell phone, take it away from him so he can't tip off his friends."

175

"I know it's fashionable in Washington to throw people in jail without charges and keep them there," said Dom, "but this isn't Washington. Here on our backward little island we usually don't toss people into the hoosegow until they commit a crime."

"How about tossing him in for interference with a police investigation?" asked the fourth man, almost genially.

"So far," said Dom, who had good reason to do exactly that, "J.W. has told you everything he knows. He isn't interfering with your investigation, he's advancing it. If I were you, I'd get to work on the evidence he's offered. I plan to do that myself."

Good old Dom.

"Since you trained professionals are on the job," I said, "I'm going home to my wife and kids."

"I'd like to see where Arbuckle died," said the fourth man. "You mind taking me there before you call it a day?"

"No problem."

"I'll follow you," he said.

I turned toward the door.

"If you think of anything else, let me know," said Dom dryly.

"I believe you have it all," I said.

Outside, the fourth man put out a hand.

"Name's Sid Roebuck," he said. He had a firm grip. So did I.

"J. W. Jackson."

"Sam Arbuckle was a friend of mine, so this is personal with me."

"It's personal with me, too, because Joe Begay is a friend of mine."

He followed me in one of the two rental cars. The winter day was short, but there was still light when we drove down my long, sandy driveway and parked in front of the house.

Roebuck got out of his car and looked around. He nodded toward the dark house. "Nobody home."

"I moved my family to another house when this business began to seem dangerous."

"I doubt if you're in any danger."

"I hope you're right." I showed him where Arbuckle's car had stopped and where he had died in my arms.

"Mind if I look in the house?"

"No."

We went in together and he went into every room. He tried the back door and looked at the windows. "You always keep the place unlocked?"

"I don't like locks."

"You keep one on the gun cabinet."

"I've got two little kids. They're not old enough to handle weapons."

"You mind giving me a look inside."

"No." I opened the cabinet and he examined its contents.

"The rifle and shotguns were my father's," I said. "The pistol is my wife's. She's a competitive shooter."

"I see you have ammunition for a couple of handguns that aren't here."

"My wife has one of her pistols, and the police have my revolver."

"Why?"

I told him about giving the .38 to Olive Otero. He grunted and shut the cabinet door.

Outside again, in the falling light, Roebuck looked at the surrounding woods and out over the brown gardens toward the cold waters of Sengekontacket Pond and Nantucket Sound, then stared up the driveway.

"You hear any shots before Sam drove down here?"

"No, but it was shotgun season, so I probably wouldn't have noticed if there was one."

"From what Sergeant Agganis said, it doesn't seem that Sam could have traveled very far after he was shot."

"He had to be tough to travel at all."

"Why do you suppose he came here to die?"

I gave him my thoughts about that, such as they were.

He nodded. "Well, we'll figure it out. You know this island and I don't. Any ideas about where to get started?"

"Nothing you and Dom Agganis haven't already thought of. I'd start asking everybody in this area if they saw or heard anything, and I'd go up every driveway and road on the off chance that I'd find the place where Arbuckle was shot. My guess is that it happened on a road that's pretty isolated, and that Arbuckle was meeting someone he knew and trusted."

"Yeah, that was my thought, too. Sam was never cynical enough for the work he did. Well, I'll be on my way. You can get in touch with me through Agganis's office if you need to. I know how to find you."

He drove away. I went inside and locked the gun cabinet, then drove to John Skye's farm. I was tired clear down to my bones.

17

Zee had picked Joshua and Diana up at school and she had a fire going in the living room fireplace. It felt good. Kisses from her and the kids felt even better, and a glass of Luksusowa on ice, adorned with a jalapeño-stuffed olive, improved things still more. She and I sat side by side on the big couch and looked at the fire. From the kitchen came the aroma of spaghetti sauce being warmed for supper.

Diana, nose busy, approached. Whatever else she was doing, Diana was always food conscious. If she was lucky, she would inherit her mother's genetic propensity to eat like a horse and never show it.

"I like this house, Pa," said our daughter.

"So do I, Diana."

"John has even more books that you do. He has a whole library."

Our computer was in the library, sitting

on the big table that served as John's desk. Diana and Joshua used the rest of the table to do their nonelectric homework.

"It's my favorite room in the whole house," I said.

"Me, too. I like our computer, but I love books more."

Like father, like daughter.

"Pa?"

"What?"

"Are we going to have our Christmas tree here? If we stay here, I think we should have our tree here, too. Christmas isn't very far away, you know."

"I don't think we need to have a tree here," I said. "We'll be in our own house very soon."

"How long, Pa?"

"I'm not sure, but not long."

"Can Santa find us if we don't have a tree?"

"Absolutely. But by Christmas we'll be back in our own house and we'll have a tree for sure. I know just where to look for one in our woods."

"Pa?"

"What?"

"Christmas is my very favorite holiday!"

"Mine, too. Now go finish your homework." I sipped my vodka. Maybe I should leave a nip for Santa, in case it was a chilly night when he popped down the chimney. I didn't like having the solstice season intruded upon by the Easter Bunny or whomever it was who had killed Samuel Arbuckle. Just as in Longfellow's day, hate was strong and mocked the song of peace on earth, goodwill to men.

"I heard about Samuel Arbuckle," said Zee, staring into the fire after little Diana had gone back to the library. "I'm glad we moved the kids here before it happened. But all I got was gossip; what's the real story?"

The Edgartown hospital is one of the island's greatest rumor mills, in part because when bad things happen on the Vineyard, the results turn up in the ER and word gets around fast. Fortunately, good news circulates almost as fast. If you want to know what's happening, in reality or someone's imagination, just talk to somebody who works at the hospital.

I told Zee about everything but Kate's hopes for a union with me. "By now," I concluded, "the DIA guys, the state police, and all ten editions of the local cops are on the case."

"Which means that you can step away from it."

"Yes."

"Good. You're getting too old for adventures."

"You're right. No more adventures for me."

We watched the flames dance just as our cave-dwelling ancestors must have done tens of thousands of years before as they sat in front of their fires.

"You have a cloud on your forehead," said Zee after a while. "What are you thinking about?"

I tried to evaporate the cloud. "Nothing," I said. I gave her a smile.

"You'd better stick to penny-ante poker," she said, "or we're liable to lose the farm."

"Nonsense. My face is stone."

"A less kindly person than I might say that you've confused your face with your brain. Why the brow?"

"I was just wondering where the Bunny is staying between murders."

"I thought you just agreed to step away from whatever it is that's going on. Besides, Arbuckle said it's not the Easter Bunny."

"That's right, but I have to call the killer by some name or other, so I'm going to keep calling him the Bunny. I'll leave off the Easter part."

"Monty Python had a man-killing bunny

in one of their shows."

"Wasn't that the Holy Grail movie? Anyway, this is a different rabbit, and he has to be living someplace on the island while he goes around murdering people. I wonder where."

Zee thought for a while. "A lot of the B-and-Bs and hotels are closed for the season. If he's staying in a place that's still open, the police will probably find out pretty fast, don't you think?"

"I imagine they'll give it a try. Any stranger will get their attention, for sure."

"And what about a car? If he's from off-island, he either brought his own car or he's rented one or stolen one since he got here."

Great minds. "The police are probably checking that out, too," I said.

"And what about a map?" asked Zee, getting into the spirit of the chase. "If he's a stranger, how does he know his way around? This island isn't very big, but it's big enough to make it hard to find where people live. How does this guy know where to prowl and keep from being noticed while he prowls? Does he ask people where to find places and other people? It seems to me that if he does, the people he asked would remember him and could tell the police what he looked like."

I put my arm around her shoulders. "Maybe you should give up nursing and join the Edgartown PD. They need a keen investigative mind like yours to think of things they never would have come up with on their own."

She snugged closer. "I'm pretty sure the Chief and Tony D'Agostine and Dom Agganis and most of the other Vineyard cops have already thought about all the things I've come up with."

True. "And maybe the Bunny has come up with them, too," I said.

She screwed her head around and looked up at me with those deep, dark eyes wherein I'd so often happily lost myself. "What do you mean?"

"I mean that if we can think of these things and the cops can think of them, the Bunny can think of them, too. In fact, he probably thought of them first, since he planned this business before putting the plan into action."

"Of course." She paused. "But how did he make a plan for a place he's never been? All he knew was that Joe Begay lived on Martha's Vineyard. Even if he knew approximately where Joe and Toni live, he wouldn't have known exactly."

185

"It isn't a secret," I said. "Kate found the house without any trouble. All she had to do was flutter her eyelashes and ask any Aquinnah cop."

"You never mentioned her eyelashes before."

Not for the first time, my mouth was right here and my common sense was way out yonder. I tightened my arm. "Hers are absolutely no challenge to yours, my sweet."

"Good. Is that how she found Joe's house?"

"Actually, I don't know how she found it, but it probably wasn't hard. And unlike the Bunny, she didn't have any reason to care whether or not she was remembered because she wasn't out to murder Joe. The Bunny would have to be more careful."

"Unless he planned to hit and run so fast that he'd be long gone before the police heard about him." We sipped our drinks and then she said, "What else have you thought about since you agreed not to think about this anymore?"

"The shotgun that killed Arbuckle. The Bunny had a shotgun. That makes me wonder if part of his plan was to take advantage of shotgun hunting season. It makes me wonder if he's a deer hunter."

"Don't they have a bow-and-arrow season first, then a shotgun season, and then a black-powder season? How long does the shotgun season last?"

"Only a week or so. It's almost over."

"Do you think he timed his arrival to correspond with the shotgun season?"

"He got close enough to Arbuckle to kill him with a shotgun. I doubt if he could have done that outside of hunting season. It could be that he was wearing an orange hunting jacket and cap. Even so, Arbuckle must have been either unsuspecting or awfully careless. His own coat wasn't even unbuttoned."

Zee thought some more, then said, "If he came down here pretending to be a hunter, do you think he bought a hunting license as part of his cover, just in case he got stopped by a warden for some reason?"

"I doubt if he'd have used his real ID to get one, but if he had fake papers, maybe so."

"He'd have used the same fake ID to rent a room or a car, wouldn't he?"

"I imagine." But I couldn't really imagine the Bunny renting either a room or a car when he got to the island. It would be too easy for the now-swarming police to find him or at least get a description of him, fake name or not.

"I think it's time for me to cook the spag," said Zee, rolling to her feet. "The water's already boiling. Din's in ten."

I followed her into Mattie Skye's kitchen. The aroma of the spaghetti sauce filled my nostrils. The old family recipe. Delish. I got the Parmesan out of the fridge and put it on the table, which was already laid, and opened the red wine.

"What I think," said Zee, "is that this bad bunny planned a very quick kill and escape, but that something went wrong. I think that Arbuckle interrupted him and that after the Bunny killed him to shut him up, he may have abandoned his plan and already be off of the island. That would be sensible, wouldn't it? Your cover is blown, so you abort the mission and save your own hide?"

"That sounds like what I would do. The other possibility is that he's still here and sticking to his plan."

She stirred the spaghetti sauce. "But where is he, then? Where's he staying? What car is he driving? How does he know how to get around the island without being noticed?"

Good questions.

"I'll call the kids," I said, but that wasn't

necessary. Diana's nose and ears had led her to supper, and her big second-grade brother was only a step behind.

The spaghetti was excellent but my thoughts were on rabbit.

18

The next morning was cold and overcast. In downtown Edgartown initial preparations were being made for the Christmas-in-Edgartown celebration, which was only a week away. The stands for the lighted trees that would line Main Street were in place, ropes and wreaths of greenery adorned with red bows were appearing on fences and doors, and candles were being placed in windows.

I cruised Main to take things in, then hooked back to Pease's Point Way and drove to the police station. There was a green wreath on the window of the locked front door. In a bow to national security policies, the station's door was now always locked in case international terrorists decided to attack. To get in, you had to push a button. I punched it and peeked through the wreath. Kit Goulart peered back from the desk and let me in.

Kit was large and pleasant. She bade me happy holidays. I returned the wish and wondered if the Chief was on the other side of his closed office door.

"He is," said Kit, "and so are some other members of the department. I believe they're organizing a hunt for the guy who shot the guy who died in your yard yesterday."

"The Chief never did like having people killed in his town," I said. "You mind telling him I'm here?"

"Not at all," said Kit, picking up a phone.

A moment later, the Chief's office door opened and a hand beckoned me in. I went in and shut the door behind me.

The room was crowded and warm. Tony D'Agostine and a half dozen other Edgartown cops were there. They nodded hello but looked pretty serious.

"We're about to go back to checking more places that take guests and rent cars," said the Chief. "You have any wise advice before we start?"

"How about places that sell hunting licenses?" I gave him Zee's theory about the Bunny being in the guise of deer hunter.

"You're a day late," said the Chief. "We

did that yesterday when we started checking hotels and inns."

"Aren't there some people who unofficially rent rooms even though they don't register with any board or organization?"

"Mostly little old ladies who can use a few extra bucks. We're checking them out." He cocked an eye at me. "Anything else you can think of? No? Okay, people, off you go." He held up a forefinger. "And be careful. If you find anything, call in; if you find anybody who looks out of place, get backup first and ask questions second."

Edgartown's finest went out of the office.

"All the towns doing this?" I asked.

"That's the master plan."

If the master plan was being followed, something good might actually come out of it because there are ten different police forces on Martha's Vineyard: one for each of the six towns, a sheriff's department, the state police, the environmental police, and the Registry of Motor Vehicles cops. And now the DIA was here, too. If all of them were working together, for a change, they could cover a lot of ground.

The Chief was eyeing me. "How you doing? It must have been bad to have

Arbuckle die in your arms like that. How's Zee taking it?"

"We're okay. I'd already moved her and the kids over to John Skye's place, so Joshua and Diana never saw anything. They'll probably know about it by tonight, though, because the news will be in the schools."

"Dom Agganis told us what's going on." He paused. "At least what he thinks is going on. He thinks that your friend Begay should go somewhere else until this is over. The woman, too. Kate MacLeod; isn't that her name?"

"I don't see either one of them following that advice."

"Maybe all the law will scare the killer off."

I shrugged. "That would be swell, all right."

He dug in a pocket and brought out his pipe and stuck it in his mouth. I once smoked a pipe and still had a rack of them at home in case I caved into the urge again. Now I only stared in envy at his ancient briar. The Chief stared back. "I'm guessing that Zee hasn't succeeded in convincing you that you can leave this business in the hands of the police," he said. "You shouldn't make promises you don't keep, you know."

I held up a hand. "I didn't make any promises. Not real ones, anyway. I may have sort of agreed that I should mind my own business, but I didn't actually promise anything."

"Your wife deserves better than you," he said. "Of course, my wife deserves better than me, too. That's true of a lot of wives, in fact. What brings you down here, anyway? Something's on your mind."

"You're still pretty friendly with Jake Spitz, aren't you? You and he got pretty close when he was down here during those summer holidays the president and his family used to make."

He chewed his pipe stem, then said, "Yeah, Jake and I still get along just fine. What about it?"

"I've been thinking about the Bunny —"

It was the Chief's turn to hold up a hand. "The Bunny? That being the Easter Bunny Agganis mentioned? Isn't he supposed to be some sort of international terrorist? But didn't Arbuckle say something to you about it not being the Bunny?"

First Zee, and now the Chief. "It's just a name I've fastened on the shooter," I said. "I don't know if the guy is the Easter Bunny, but I have to call him something, so I'm calling him the Bunny. Maybe I should call him George Washington or Captain Marvel, but I'm calling him the Bunny. Is that okay?"

"Don't get huffy," said the Chief. "Call him whatever you damn please. Anyway, what about him?"

"I've been thinking that maybe he isn't staying in an inn or a hotel."

The Chief frowned. "Then where is he staying? In a tent? In some house he broke into?"

"It could be, but I don't think so. I think he may be staying with a friend or even in his own house."

The Chief took his pipe out of his mouth and looked at it for a while. "Go on," he said.

"Here's the thought," I said. "There are a good many Washington people who have houses on this island, including old Yalies and other IC types. McNamara, Kennedy, and Johnson are names that come to mind. They all rented or bought land here at one time or another, and you probably know the names of other bigwigs that I don't, what with national security being so popular these days and even you small-town cops being in on it."

"So far," said the Chief, "all Washington has given us is more work for no more money. What's your point?"

"My point is this: What if Arbuckle was right? What if it isn't the Easter Bunny or any other foreign agent who's doing these killings? What if it's somebody else, somebody with an agenda of his own? An American with a grudge."

The Chief poked at the bowl of his pipe, tamping down the remains of a previous smoke. "You think it might be somebody in the IC?"

"It makes sense, since the dead people were all in that game and so are Joe Begay and Kate MacLeod, although they'll both deny it officially."

He nodded. "Somebody in the IC who has a house on the Vineyard or has a friend who has one."

I nodded back. "Maybe a house with a car in the garage?"

"A private house and car would make it a lot easier for him," he said. "And if it's his own house, it would explain why he knows his way around the island. If he's a hunter, it might even explain where he got his shotgun."

The Chief opened a drawer, got out a package of tobacco, and filled his pipe bowl. I inhaled the scent of the tobacco. Mighty fine!

"And if he was someone Arbuckle knew and trusted," I said, "it would explain why he was able to get close with the shotgun."

The Chief stuck the pipe back in his mouth and I knew that he wanted to light up but wouldn't because he only smoked outside. "I imagine this line of thought has occurred to the Feds," he said. "These DIA guys aren't idiots."

"You're probably right," I said, "although being an idiot is no bar to government employment, so you may be wrong. What I think is that it would be a good idea for you to call Jake Spitz and see if he can get a line on anybody who smells wrong."

"You mean like somebody in the IC who has a house on Martha's Vineyard and has taken a vacation during the past week?"

"By Jove, I think you've got it!"

He shook his head. "Do you have any idea how many people in Washington take vacations during the Christmas season? Even if you could limit it to IC people who own houses on the Vineyard or have friends who do, I can't imagine Jake Spitz or anybody else getting a line on that many people."

I pulled a sheet of paper out of my pocket and handed it to him. "Have him start with this list."

He looked at the paper. "Who are these people?"

"That's a list of all the names I've heard since I got involved with this business. The starred names are the dead people. If Spitz takes this job, I imagine he'll start looking at their friends and colleagues. Some people probably already have. Several of those names belong to guys, both dead and alive, who were Kate MacLeod's lovers, or so she says."

"There's so much easy sex around these days that you'd think nobody would get mad enough to kill over it," said the Chief, "but that's not the case. People are strange."

Nobody knows that better than a cop.

"All right," said the Chief. "I'll give Spitz a call. But don't expect too much. By the way, I join your wife in suggesting that you leave this business to the police. We'll all be happier. How cold is it outside?"

"Chilly."

He got up. "I'll just step out for a short smoke."

"Smoking is bad for you."

"So are you," he said, and followed me out the front door. "Why didn't you just call Spitz yourself? You two are pretty close to being friends."

"I thought the voice of authority might swing more weight. Let me know if you learn anything."

"I might. What's keeping your nose stuck to this smelly affair?"

"Joe Begay is a friend of mine."

He brought out his ancient Zippo and lit up.

"Friendship can be a complicated business," he said between puffs. "A lot of murderers and their victims were friends. Sam Arbuckle might attest to that if he could talk."

19

Back at our house, I went through the rooms and verified that no one had tossed the place since I'd left. Maybe I really should get some locks, although they wouldn't do much good against a pro. I thought of the poisoned needles in Kate's bed and reading chair, and looked uneasily at my own upholstery and bedding, but there was no sign of any disturbance of any kind.

What a way to get killed: by sitting or lying on a needle. I wondered once again if as much human ingenuity was expended on helping people as on harming them. Once, long ago, after several beers, I'd broached the same question to a friend just home from a trip to England. He had answered it by contrasting the armor collection in the Tower of London with the nonviolent scientific devices that filled the museum at Greenwich.

When I went to London, he said, I could go to both museums and decide the question to my own satisfaction.

But I still haven't been to London and still don't know.

I checked the gun cabinet and found all our weapons in place. Why shouldn't they be, since the Bunny already had his own shotgun?

I watered our indoor plants, then refilled the food and water dishes belonging to Oliver Underfoot and Velcro before schmoozing with them for a while. They, like most cats, pretended to be above the need for human companionship but actually were very social in their catty way. Oliver wrapped himself around my ankles as was his wont, and Velcro buzzed in my lap when I carefully sat in my Archie Bunker chair and dialed Joe Begay's cell phone number.

When Joe answered I said I wanted to see him and hung up before anyone could trace the call. Actually, I didn't know anything about how long it took to trace calls, but I figured the less time I was on the line, the less likely the trace.

My technological knowledge and skills were clearly far out-of-date, and I wondered yet again if I should do something about it. Maybe. On the other hand, maybe not, because the prospect of spending much time learning things that didn't interest me failed to inspire me, even though the knowledge would clearly be to my advantage as I engaged the world.

The thing was, I didn't want to engage the world. I had come to Martha's Vineyard precisely to become disengaged, to get away.

But of course, there is no away, as my present circumstances proved.

As I drove to Aquinnah, snow began to fall. A light mist hung close to the ground and it, combined with the falling snow and the contrast between the snow-covered ground and the dark, leafless trees, gave the island an almost ethereal appearance. On either side of the road I could see into the woods, but couldn't tell exactly how far, and I was reminded of Bev Doolittle paintings, where the spotted horses blend and become one with the snow and trees.

It was akin to sailing through fog in a light wind: there's a circle of sight around your boat, but it's impossible to know whether the space is a few yards in diameter or half a mile.

I passed parked pickups and wondered if

it was still shotgun season or whether the hunters were now using black powder. Did the Bunny own a muzzle-loader that would allow him to walk up to his next victim as he must have walked up to Arbuckle?

A snowy mist hung over Menemsha Pond and around the tops of the Aquinnah hills. The old Land Cruiser's heater hadn't been much good for a long time, and I was chilly as I drove.

I turned right toward Lobsterville, then left onto Lighthouse Road. Off to my right was Dogfish Bar, where once you could find easy parking and easy access to one of the island's prime spots for bass, but where now parking was hard to find and new landowners preferred that fishermen stay away.

So things go.

I turned in to Uncle Bill Vanderbeck's house and parked. Kate's rental car was gone, but Bill's old Ford was there. Where was Kate?

There were boot tracks in the snow, leading from the barn to the house. I went to the front door, knocked, and heard Joe's voice telling me to come in.

The room was comfortably warm after my chilly ride in the truck. Joe turned from a window and waved at the stove. He had a steaming cup in his hand.

"Help yourself to some coffee."

I did that and we sat in two of Uncle Bill's comfortable old chairs.

"Any news?" I asked.

Joe shook his head. "No, but he'll come. Soon, I think. He's already been on the island too long for his own safety."

"Maybe. Were you over at your house when I called?"

"Yes, but never mind that. If he shows up there while I'm here, I'll see his tracks when I go back. What brings you here?"

"I want you to tell me about the first mission you did with Kate. You and she and Susan Bancroft and a guy named Stephen Harkness were the team. You told me you trusted her because of that job."

"Yes."

"Even though she'd slept with Stephen? That sort of thing usually causes trouble."

He nodded. "It usually does, but part of Kate's genius is that she may leave them sad, but they're rarely mad. They're mostly grateful, in fact. Besides, I wasn't heading that mission. Susan was, and she put Stephen in his place when he came on to her. She didn't have a problem with whatever had passed between him and Kate, but she wanted none of Stephen herself."

"How did Stephen take it?"

"He was our communications man, and he didn't like it when Susan sent him back to his own bedroll, but it didn't keep him from doing his job."

"How did he feel when Kate made a play for you? Because, knowing Kate, she surely did."

Begay's hawk face showed no expression, but his dark eyes gleamed. "I told her I was unavailable, and she went away from me."

"And how did she take it?"

"She took it well enough for me to accept her later as part of the trade mission. As I just said, Kate's private life has never intruded on her work."

"What went wrong on the first mission? I know that Stephen was badly injured."

He thought for a while, deciding what to tell me, if anything. Then he said, "The job was done, but we had to get past one more checkpoint on our way out. Kate, Susan, and I had good papers, but Stephen had lost his somewhere along the line, so we sent him through the brush while the rest of us diverted the guards' attention at the checkpoint.

"Kate and Susan sweet-talked the corporal of the guard and I gave cigarettes to the squad that manned the post. Everything seemed fine, but the corporal spotted Stephen and one of the soldiers shot him. He was hit badly, but we got him over the hill to the cars that were waiting and to a hospital and eventually back to the States." He paused. "He doesn't have much control over what happens below his waist, but he lived."

"What about the guards at the checkpoint?"

He shrugged. "There were only the three privates and the corporal, and they were all looking at Stephen."

"You killed them?"

He gave another shrug, but said nothing.

"What became of Stephen after he got Stateside?"

"The IC takes care of its own. He got an office job that doesn't require legs. He still had his security clearance, so he was a valuable asset." His lips tightened. "I heard that his wife had to be institutionalized when she first learned what had happened to him. This kind of work can be hard on the women at home."

I could attest to that. My first wife left me because she couldn't bear the pressure of being married to a cop and never knowing if I'd come home alive. Her second husband was a schoolteacher who offered her a less stressful life.

I drank and thought and said, "How did he happen to lose his papers?"

"Ah," said Joe, "that very question came up during debriefing, but there was never an official finding. Lost, strayed, or stolen are the three possibilities. We had some hectic times on that job, and anything could have happened."

"Stolen?"

"We worked with native assets we didn't get to choose. Some of them probably weren't above putting their hands into our packs if they had a chance. It's even possible that some of the target's agents were mixed in with ours."

"What did Stephen think?"

"They debriefed him at the hospital. I'm told that he favored theft. Of course, that's exactly what he could be expected to say. If he had just lost the papers, what happened to him would be his own fault."

"What do you think?"

"All I know is that Stephen had bad luck at the checkpoint. If that corporal had been looking at Kate and Susan like his buddies were and like he had every reason to, he never would have spotted Stephen."

My coffee was cooling. I sipped some more of it.

"Who headed up the second mission, the trade mission?"

"I did."

"Did you get to select the people who went with you?"

"Mostly. I suppose that if the Boss really wanted somebody in particular to go, I'd have taken him; but that didn't happen; I chose the people I wanted."

"And you chose Edo and Kate along with Francis and Susan. Had you worked with Francis and Edo before?"

"No, but I'd heard of them and I talked with people who knew them as well as you can know anybody in this business."

"But later Susan OD'd. Was she a drug addict when she was on the trade mission?"

"Susan wasn't an addict," said Begay. "She was murdered. Somebody shot her up after she was unconscious."

"Do you think Edo was murdered?"

"Edo was killed on a mission. I don't know if anybody murdered him."

"How about Francis?"

Begay's smile was less sardonic than sad. "The story is that he happened to be in a deli when it was robbed, and he got shot by a kid with a habit who got himself arrested less than a block away. There's irony for you. You work dangerous jobs in dangerous parts of the world and you come home and get killed down the street from your apartment when you go to get a pound of salami."

I studied him over the rim of my cup. "One murder doesn't add up to revenge killings by the Easter Bunny."

"What I know is that there are only three of us left from my last two overseas jobs: Kate, me, and Stephen Harkness. And that it wasn't an accident that killed Arbuckle."

"I talked to the Chief in Edgartown this morning. I asked him to have Jake Spitz check out the names I've gotten from you and Kate."

"Good."

"Have the DIA people been in touch with you?"

"This morning. They're not happy about Arbuckle. I don't think I was much help to them." He glanced at his watch. "I'm going to check out my house. Do you want to come along?"

"I'm not carrying."

"Here." He magically produced a smallish pistol. "My backup gun. It's a Kahr P40. Double-action, no safety, six-shot magazine and one in the chamber. You point and pull the trigger." He put it in my hand. "Shall we go?"

"Yes. Should I take my car?"

"We'll walk. I see you're wearing your Bean boots, so you should be fine."

The snow had stopped falling. We walked to the barn. We went in the front door and out the back door and into the woods. There was a thin layer of fresh snow over the older snow beneath our feet and on the needles of the evergreen trees. We walked in silence for twenty minutes, then Begay put out a hand and gestured downward. I knelt in the snow and looked ahead.

There, through the trees, I could see Joe's house, with Toni's snow-covered car parked in front of it. Joe pointed and I looked at the driveway and saw tire tracks.

20

The tracks were of a car that had driven in, turned around, and left. Footprints led from the car tracks to the front door of the house, then around the house, then from the house around Toni's car and back to the tracks of the unknown car.

Hmmmm.

"Fresh," said Joe. "I was here when I got your call and this has happened since."

"Could be friend or foe," I said. "Any chance that somebody's stashed in the house, waiting for you to show up?"

"Not unless he wears the same boots as the guy who got back in the car and drove away."

"He has small feet," I said.

"Most people have small feet compared to ours," said Joe.

True. When I danced, I was a serious threat to my partner's feet, and Joe's boots were at least as big as mine.

I studied the tracks, then said, "Why don't I go out to the end of the driveway and see if anybody's hanging around?"

"Do that."

I went through the cold trees, over the thin snow, out to the road. The snow showed that the car had come from the direction of the lighthouse and had returned the same way. It was gone. The road was empty. I knelt for a while, slowly moving only my head as I studied the road and the trees on either side of it.

Nobody.

Nothing.

I looked some more, then went back to the house, my breath making gray clouds in the winter air.

Joe's footprints led from the trees to the front door, then around the house as he followed the prints of his visitor.

Not eager to have him mistake me for someone else, I called his name as I, too, went around the house. He was looking at a rear window.

"Anything?" I asked.

He shook his head. "No. All my markers are still there."

We went on around the house and he checked every window. No one had entered.

"Maybe it was just a neighbor looking for you," I said. "Or maybe somebody who was looking for Toni, wondering why she hasn't been around lately."

"Maybe."

"Maybe it was Kate."

"Not unless her feet have grown."

We walked out to Toni's car. The visitor had brushed snow from the driver's-side window and had created a confusion of footprints around the car.

I wondered if it was locked and reached for the door handle.

"I wouldn't do that," said Joe sharply.

I took my hand away.

He got down on his knees and looked under the car, then moved to a new spot and looked again. He repeated this until he seemed satisfied with his search. He stood and looked at the car from all sides.

"Cute," he said.

"Cute?"

"The snow was falling when he was here. He took a chance that it would keep falling and cover up his work. But it stopped."

"And?"

"And so we step back into the trees a ways. Maybe we can turn this into something useful to us. It'll cost, but it might make him careless. Come on."

213

I followed him into the woods for fifty yards, until we stopped under a barren oak.

"This should be far enough," he said. "You know what this is?" He showed me a small black device taken from his pocket.

What a question. "No. I see ads in the *Globe* for gadgets that do high-tech things teenagers understand, but I don't know one from another."

"You should try to get with the times, J.W. This really isn't anything new or high-tech; it's a fairly old gimmick. What it does is start your car from a distance, so it'll be warmed up by the time you get in."

"You want Toni's car warmed up?"

"Not exactly," said Joe. "In fact, I hope I'm wrong about this. Get behind that tree."

I did and he pushed a button on the device.

The explosion tore a hole in the air. A few small branches detached themselves from their trees and fell down around us.

I found that I had thrown myself flat onto the snowy earth. I pushed myself up. Joe brushed a twig off his shoulder.

"I was afraid of that," he said. "Toni is going to be very angry."

"Only after she knows you're still alive," I said.

"I hope you're right," said Joe. "Now we'll go back and sit in the woods awhile so we can see who shows up. That blast should have been heard for at least a couple of miles."

We walked back until we could see the house and the flaming car. The front windows of the house had been blown in and a bench on the front porch had been ripped into two pieces.

We watched as Toni's car burned and melted the snow all around it. Broken branches and little piles of brown dirt were strewn over the remaining snow in the parking area. Seeing this, I remembered the flying pieces of trees and undergrowth and body parts that had been the result of the long-ago mortar barrage that had decimated my first and last wartime patrol, and I realized I was trembling.

"Now, we wait," said Joe, sitting on his heels.

I knelt beside him.

Time passed.

The explosion had been so loud it seemed that half the citizens of Aquinnah should have heard it and come to investigate, but no one came.

More time passed. The car burned silently, sending smoke into the misty air.

It started to snow again. Who can fathom Mother Nature's moods?

The snow fell and fell, and we waited and waited.

The snow began to fill the car tracks and footprints, but the fiery car melted anything that fell near it.

Then a car came down the driveway. It was Mercedes-Benz's pricy contribution to the SUV market. Half the people on Martha's Vineyard had four-wheel-drive vehicles, but not many of them owned a Mercedes-Benz. The SUV stopped well back from the flaming ruins of Toni's car, and the driver stepped out and stared, then hurried as close as he could get and peered into the flames.

I didn't recognize him, and Joe said nothing. The man pulled a cell phone from his pocket, dialed a number and spoke, then went back to his car and pulled it to one side of the driveway before returning to the site of the explosion. He looked hard into the remains of the car, then went to the house and looked in through broken windows. Over the sound of the fire I heard his voice: "Hello! Anybody in there? Hello!"

Joe Begay sat as unmoving and silent as a stone.

Then, in the distance, I heard the sound of a siren, and not much later a fire truck came into the yard, followed by two pickups that were quickly joined by another. Aquinnah's volunteer firemen went quickly to work.

Joe touched my arm and nodded back toward the direction we had come, and the two of us scuttled away through the woods. Halfway to Uncle Bill Vanderbeck's house, Joe said, "We'll take your truck and drive in as though we just came home and saw the commotion. Do you know the guy in the Mercedes?"

"No. Do you?"

"No, but I got the license plate number."

So had I. "We can ask who he is when we get there," I said. "Where have we been driving?"

"We were out looking for Kate."

When we got to my old Land Cruiser we drove toward Joe's house but, to prevent anyone tracing our tracks back to Uncle Bill's place, drove up and around the loop leading to the cliffs and came back to Joe's driveway. We pulled in and stopped behind the last of the half dozen pickups and trucks that were now on the scene.

Joe walked in front of me, looking this way and that. When he came to the first of the firemen, he said, "What's going on?"

"Car fire, Joe. Pretty much under control now."

The fire chief came to us. "Anybody home here, Joe? Toni or the kids?"

Joe shook his head. "No. They're away. What happened?"

"Too soon to say." He gestured toward the driver of the Mercedes. "This fella says he heard what sounded like an explosion then saw smoke and came here and called us."

Joe looked at the man. "Explosion?"

"That's what he says. Says he was up on the cliffs, on the lookout there, when he heard the sound and saw the smoke. Near as we can tell, Joe, there was nobody in the car. You have a gasoline leak or anything?"

"No. Anybody else hear an explosion?"

"A couple of the guys here say they might have, but didn't think much of it, being as how it's hunting season and guns are going off in the woods. Happened about a half hour ago, near as I can figure."

"Who's the guy?"

The chief got out a notebook. "Name's Stuart Oakland. Here for the holidays. Got a house down in Oak Bluffs. You don't know him, I take it."

"No."

"Well, he did the right thing. If we'd had a north wind, the fire might have touched off the house. We haven't been in there yet, by the way. You want to let us in? Just to make sure no sparks made it inside."

"Sure." Joe led him to the door, unlocked it, and stepped inside. The fire chief followed.

I stayed where I was and took a good look at Stuart Oakland. He must be the son of Professor Buford Oakland, whose house I had opened a few days back in Oak Bluffs. He was a handsome man in his midthirties, clean-shaven and dressed in expensive-looking winter clothing. I wondered if he'd been named after Lee's general. It seemed possible, given his father's enthusiasm for the Civil War.

21

I walked over to Oakland and put out my hand. He took it and I could feel restrained strength in his grip.

"I'm J. W. Jackson," I said. "I opened up your house for your father a few days back. I hope everything is satisfactory."

Close up, I could see that his face and hands were tanned from some recent time in a summer sun. On the ring finger of his left hand was a golden ring studded with a single diamond only slightly smaller than my head. His eyes were blue beneath hooded lids. His lips formed a smile.

"Ah, so you're Mr. Jackson. My father gave me your name and phone number, in case something was wrong in the house. Nothing is, by the way. I'm Stuart Oakland."

"My friends call me J.W."

"And mine call me Stu. Quite a coincidence that we should meet under these circumstances. Are you a friend of the man who lives here?"

"Joe Begay and I have known each other a long time."

"Have you?" He nodded toward the smoking car. "Quite a fire. Any idea what happened?"

"No. Joe and I just got here. The fire chief says you heard an explosion and saw the smoke from up on the cliffs. You see anybody around when you got here?"

He shook his head. "Not a soul. I phoned nine-one-one as soon as I saw the car. The firemen were here very quickly. I stayed in case they wanted to debrief me. So far nobody's asked me much, not that there's much to tell."

"You're in the military?"

He cocked a brow. "What makes you ask?"

"Debrief isn't a usual civilian term."

He laughed easily. "No, I'm not in the military. It's a term you hear around Washington, where I work. I guess I just picked it up somewhere along the line."

I thrust my hands into the pockets of my coat. "It's a chilly time for a Southerner to be coming north for a holiday."

He returned his own hands to his coat

pockets. "I got used to New England weather when I was at Yale, and I have a friend here who keeps an iceboat on Squibnocket Pond. We plan to get out there if the ice is thick enough."

The idea of being cold for fun didn't appeal to me. It was one of the reasons I'd given up duck shooting. Duck shooters love terrible weather. The worse it is, the more they like it. After shivering in blinds with my shotgun for several seasons, I'd finally realized that sitting in front of a warm fire with a glass of cognac and a good book was much more enjoyable. Nowadays when I wanted wild duck, I'd buy it from some hunter friend who still enjoyed freezing half to death between shots.

"Your folks coming up for Christmas?" I asked.

Another headshake. "Not this year. I've got the place to myself. Shall I let you know when I leave? I actually expect to pull out before Christmas. Friends in Georgetown have an annual solstice party that I hate to miss."

In every nation north of the equator people celebrated and gave thanks for the end of lengthening nights and the slow growth of daylight. Thanks to the efforts of the priests and priestesses and to the gods who accepted their petitions, death by ice was averted once again and life was renewed. Christ was born; the New Year's baby replaced the bent old man; Osiris was made new; the old king was dead, long live the new king! Deck the halls.

"Give me a call when you're ready to pull out," I said. "What sort of work do you do when you're not iceboating and celebrating the Yule? Are you an academic like your father?"

He gave me a studying look, then changed it to a smile. "No, I'm just a government paper shuffler, I'm afraid. I represent your tax dollars at work. How about you? I hear it's not easy to make a living here during the winter."

"I'm a fisherman," I said. "Right now I'm scalloping. And I look after a few houses like your father's."

"Tough job, fishing. Must be cold out there on the water this time of year."

"Cold enough, but that's where the scallops are."

He made a sympathetic sound. "I don't mind having fun in the cold, but I prefer my nice warm office for work."

"You sound like a duck hunter," I said.

"I've popped a cap or two. How'd you guess?"

"They freeze for fun, just like you iceboaters. No surprise, I guess. I once heard a woman who took people on river-rafting trips say that people will pay a lot of money to be miserable."

He laughed. "That's probably true, now that I think about it."

Joe and the fire chief came out of the house. I put out my hand to Oakland once again. "Well, nice meeting you. Maybe we'll see each other again."

"Under happier circumstances, I hope." We smiled at each other and I went over to where Joe was looking at a broken window and saying to the chief, "I'll put some plywood over these until I can replace the glass."

"I can go get it right now," I said. "You don't need me here."

As I drove to Cottle's lumberyard on Lambert's Cove Road, I thought things over. At the yard I tied sheets of half-inch plywood onto the top of the truck. On my way back to Aquinnah, I thought some more.

All communities are small communities. Their citizens, however different in social status or condition, know one another and share common problems and blessings. The Vineyard, diverse as it was in landscape and inhabitants, was at the same time a small community with shared conditions, concerns, conflicts, and interests. As was reflected in the letters to the editors of the island papers, not much happened that didn't inspire readers to write paeans of praise or diatribes of condemnation.

I didn't know much about the gigantic U.S. intelligence community, but I was willing to bet that it was small in spite of its size; that events and personalities were widely known, and that letters and opinions pertaining to them were produced with the same passion as was found in Vineyard newspapers.

The difference was that the IC exchanges were often hidden from public view on grounds of national security, that catchall term that all too often actually serves less to guard the country than to cover government asses.

The need for national security notwithstanding, the IC didn't exist in isolation, and IC people were not that different from other people. Their jobs might involve high security, but there was more to them than their jobs. They had families, mortgages, triumphs, and problems like everyone else.

Samuel Arbuckle had a family; Kate MacLeod had a very active social life; Joe Begay spent most of his time with his wife and children on Martha's Vineyard. None of these activities and interests had anything to do with their work.

Except, perhaps, for Kate's private life. It involved other IC people sometimes, at least, and both the FBI and the DIA were probably already investigating those connections.

Everyone seemed to know everyone else. Arbuckle knew Stephen Harkness, who slept with Kate, who also slept with Edo, Francis, and others I didn't know of.

I wished I knew more about all those people. Who hated whom; who was married to whom; who knew what. Who killed Arbuckle and Susan and placed the needles in Kate's flat. Where the Easter Bunny was, and where the killer who wasn't the Bunny was.

Kate seemed to be at the center of things. Where was she? The last time I'd seen her she'd been half joking about going to a bar to pick up a man for the night. Had she gone?

What little I knew about the IC I'd

learned from my Internet search. Maybe there was a site that would tell me what I needed to know about the people on my list.

I wondered how I could find it.

I wondered where Kate was.

I thought about Stuart Oakland and his father. Little gears were trying to turn in my brain but were failing to get the machine running. My mind was like an old car on a cold day: slow to turn over; reluctant to start.

Back at Joe's house the burned-out car was only a bad-smelling hulk and most of the volunteer firemen had gone back to their regular jobs. Stuart Oakland had also departed. A fire marshal was going to have the job of figuring out what had happened. My advice to Joe, as he brought out his circular saw, hammer, and nails and we went to work cutting the plywood and nailing pieces of it over the broken windows, was to admit nothing about his part in the blast.

Joe allowed as how he'd already thought of that. "I've been using Uncle Bill Vanderbeck's Ford lately," he said, "so I still have all the wheels I need."

"How long has Kate been gone?" I asked.

He frowned. "She didn't come home last night, but she called from some bar and told me that might happen and not to worry. I haven't seen her today. Jesus, it's like she's fifteen years old and I'm her father."

"She'll probably show up. She's a big girl and she knows what she's doing. She can handle herself if she needs to."

I nodded toward the burned-out car. "Well, at least we know that Bunny is still around. What did you think of Stuart Oakland being Johnny-on-the-spot?"

"I wish the snow hadn't covered up those first tire tracks. I'd liked to have compared them to the ones his Mercedes makes."

"You think he wired that bomb?"

"Everybody's a suspect. The only reason you're off the list is that you were with me when whoever did it, did it."

"How do you know it wasn't done earlier?"

"Because I come down here every day and start the car from out in the woods. It never blew up until today."

"It's nice to be innocent," I said, driving in a final nail. "Did Kate mention what bar she was in?"

"No, but it was noisy." He looked at the

remains of the car. "Whoever set this blast knows more than most people."

"Ex-military?"

He nodded. "Could be. But maybe he learned how to do it from the Internet. You can learn how to build atomic bombs on the Internet."

"What now?"

"Now you go home and I stay here and try to find out a little more about how this job was done."

"I don't need this anymore," I said, and handed him the little Kahr P40 he'd loaned me. "You want me to hang around and give you a ride back to the house?"

"No, thanks. I'll walk."

So I left him there and drove to Oak Bluffs.

22

There are only two towns on Martha's Vineyard where you can buy liquor: Oak Bluffs and Edgartown. The other five towns are, wisely, some say, dry. If you want to get drunk or have wine with your dinner in them, you have to bring your own bottle. As might be guessed, most of the island's fights are between drunks overindulging in Oak Bluffs and Edgartown. Maybe that's why the county jail is in Edgartown: it's convenient to the action.

Since Edgartown prides itself on being wealthy and proper, the police work hard at keeping the bars relatively quiet. Oak Bluffs, on the other hand, is openly noisy, especially along Circuit Avenue, the main drag, which sports several bars and restaurants. Young people prefer to hang out in Oak Bluffs, rather than in the other towns, because of its sound and activity, and the town makes a lot of money off them. So as long as things don't get too tempestuous, the Oak Bluffs cops just smile and stay alert.

I figured that if Kate had called from a noisy bar, it had probably been one in Oak Bluffs. All of the island's bars are filled with strangers during tourist season, but since it was now December, I thought there was a possibility that a bartender or a waitress might remember a gorgeous Anglo-Asian woman such as Kate.

I started looking for her at Offshore Ale, the island's only brew pub. Its home-brewed beers and ales are excellent and it also offers its patrons decent pub food, a dartboard, and a lot of music.

"Haven't seen you lately, J.W.," said Elvira when I came in. "What'll it be?"

"I'm looking for a woman," I said.

"You already have a woman," said Elvira, "but if Zee isn't enough for you, how about adding me? I'll stick Henry with the kids and you and I can go to Hawaii or some other warm place. What do you say?"

"I'm too old to run off with you," I said. "You'd ruin me within a week and then Zee would be mad at me and Christmas would be spoiled for my kids."

"Just trying to help out," said Elvira.

231

"You can help out by telling me if the woman I'm looking for was in here last night." I described Kate.

Elvira shook her head. "Sounds like she'd be hard to miss. Nobody like that was here last night."

"I'll keep hunting," I said, heading for the door. "Maybe Henry will take you to Hawaii."

"Ha! He's bought one of those gigantic TVs and he won't leave home until the NFL play-offs are over and the Super Bowl's been played!"

I went down to the foot of Circuit Avenue and started back up the street, hitting the bars in succession. In the first two nobody could remember having seen anyone who looked like Kate. Then I came to the Fireside and my luck changed.

The Fireside is not the classiest bar on the island, but before I got married and settled down, it had been one of my favorites. It is the haunt of some of the seedier locals and smells of beer and cigarettes and, more faintly, of marijuana, although smoking either tobacco or weed is officially illegal in public places.

Opposite the bar, along the wall, is a row of booths with knife-marked tables. The farthest of these booths is known to

232

regulars as the Confessional because some peculiar quirk of construction allows people in the next booth to hear everything that's said within it. Newcomers, especially young lovers, are steered there by jesters in need of entertainment with their beer.

My friend Bonzo worked at the Fireside, sweeping floors, bringing beer up from the cellar, serving drinks, wiping tables, cleaning up spills, and otherwise performing those simple but necessary tasks required in any bar. Their simplicity was exactly challenging enough to keep him attentive, for Bonzo had long ago fried some essential part of his brain with bad acid and had been transformed from a promising lad into an eternal child, sweet and gentle, the sad apple of his mother's eye.

Now, in midafternoon, the place was almost empty. I waved at Bonzo, who was pushing his broom, sat down at the bar, and ordered a Sam Adams.

"Long time no see," said the bartender. "A lot of married guys keep right on coming in after they get hitched, but not you."

"Home is the place for me," I said. "I've spent enough time in bars to last me the rest of my life. You on duty last night?"

"Nope, I was home in front of my fireplace. Nicki was tending bar."

"I'm looking for a woman," I said. "She might have been here last night."

He gestured. "Bonzo was here. Maybe he can help you."

"Okay with you if I buy him a beer?"

"Why not?"

I beckoned to Bonzo and he came over, a smile on his innocent face.

"Hey, J.W., how you doing?"

"Good. I'm buying you a beer. Your boss, here, said it was okay."

Bonzo looked doubtful. "You sure? I got work to do, you know. I can't be drinking on the job."

"It's a special occasion," said the bartender, putting a Sam in front of him. "A sort of Christmas present from the management."

"Gee, thanks." Bonzo climbed onto the stool beside mine. "I like beer, you know, but I can't drink much of it. It makes my head go around."

I touched his glass with mine. "Cheers."

"Cheers to you, too, J.W."

We drank and I told him whom I was looking for and how she looked, and said, "She may have been in here last night. You see anybody like that?"

He beamed. "You know something, J.W.?

I sure did see her. She's not very big but she sure is a pretty girl. I liked looking at her and — you know what? — she smiled at me!"

"What time was she here, Bonzo? Do you remember?"

He thought about the question but then shook his head. "It wasn't too late, but I don't know exactly when it was. I know she and the man were gone before we closed up because I kept looking at her, you know, and one time I looked and she was gone. Sorry, J.W. I should have looked at my watch, maybe." He showed me his watch. It, like mine, was the under-ten-dollars kind.

"That's okay, Bonzo. Tell me about the man. Did you know him?"

"Oh no. I never seen him before. He was a stranger, just like her. These days, you know, we have strangers around almost all year. It's not like it used to be when off-island people only mostly came in the summer. Now they come down earlier every year and stay later." He looked into my face. "It's what they call the shoulder seasons, you know. Like the shoulders on a man. They're getting wider all the time, so we have strangers here all the way to New Year's these days. He was one of them, and so was she."

"Did you happen to hear his name?"

He thought some more, then shook his head. "No, I never did. And I guess I never heard her name either because if I'd heard it, I'd remember it. I sure wouldn't forget the name of a girl as pretty as she is."

"If it's the same woman, her name is Kate. If she comes back, maybe you should ask her."

He blushed. "Oh, I don't know if I could just go up to her and do that. I don't think I could just go up and ask her if she's named Kate. Gee, no, I don't think so."

"What did the man look like?"

His brow furrowed as he thought back. "Well," he said finally, "he looked like he was glad to see Kate."

"You mean they didn't come in together?"

"Oh no. She came in first and then he came in and pretty soon they were sitting together over in that booth there, laughing and talking like they was old friends. I could tell that some of the other guys were getting ready to go talk with her themselves, but then the man came in and he talked with her first and after that, nobody else talked with her. Just the man."

"Can you describe him? You know: Was

he tall or short? Young or old? Did he have a beard? What color was his hair, if he had any? What kind of clothes was he wearing?"

"Oh, I get what you mean, J.W. Let me think." More furrows, then his brow smoothed. "He was what you'd call medium. Not tall, not short, not young, not old. Sort of as old as you are, maybe; you know what I mean? He was wearing winter clothes just like everybody else, and you know what?" He held up a forefinger and smiled happily. "I remember for sure that he didn't have a mustache or a beard because when I brought them their drinks, he didn't have either one! And you know what else I saw?"

"What?"

"I saw her talking once on one of those little telephones everybody has. I'd like to have one of those myself, J.W., so I could just call somebody whenever I wanted to."

That might have been her call to Joe Begay. "What were they drinking?" I asked. "Can you remember?"

His professional pride appeared. "Heck, yes, J.W. I work here in this bar, you know, and I have to remember what people are drinking! They were both drinking bourbon and water. Ladies don't usually

237

drink bourbon, but that's what she was drinking. They both had several before they left."

"How'd they seem to be getting along?"

"They were getting along good, J.W. They were talking and laughing and having a good time. And I think they were still happy when they left because they left a big tip like happy people do."

After I left the Fireside, I spent an hour going into all of the other bars in town, but no one else had seen Kate or her companion.

Where had they gone? Who was the man?

I drove to Edgartown and parked in front of the police station. Kit Goulart buzzed me in, then rang the Chief to see if he was free to see me. I went to his office and told him most of the truth about what had happened to Toni Begay's car, leaving out only the part about Joe and me being in the woods when Joe pressed the button that detonated the explosives. Then I told him about Kate being out of touch and about my talk with Bonzo.

"You've had a busy day," he said.

"How about your day?" I asked. "Did you find out anything about the guys on the list I gave you?"

"What I found out is police business."

"Here I tell you everything and you won't tell me anything."

"That's right."

"Hell of a note."

"If you're going to cry, I'll give you a tissue."

I looked at the computer on his desk. "If you found anything out, you did it awfully fast. Did you use that thing?"

"What if I did? Modern technology is a tool of modern law enforcement. Too bad you're still living in the last century, otherwise even you could probably find out things you want to know." He leaned back and put his hands behind his neck.

"Are you telling me that the information I want is there on the Internet?"

"I'm not telling you anything."

"How do I find it?"

"You probably can't, because you're not as computer smart as me or your children or your wife."

Hmmmm.

I looked at my watch. In not too long, Zee and the kids would be at John Skye's house. "Well," I said, getting up, "it's been great talking with you."

"The pleasure has been all mine," said his voice as I went out the door.

23

I was sitting in John Skye's library staring at the computer screen when Zee came home with Joshua and Diana. I went out to meet them.

Zee's nose was twitching both before and after my kiss.

"What's cooking, chef?"

I checked the fire in the fireplace. It was burning nicely. "I'm heating kale soup," I said. "I stopped at home and got some, along with a loaf of bread."

"Ah. Winter security is a supply of kale soup in the freezer."

She went off to change out of her hospital clothes while I learned that my children had had a reasonably enjoyable day at their schools, even though thoughts of the coming holidays were beginning to intrude upon scholarly activities.

"We wanted to talk about Christmas,"

said Diana, "but our teacher said it wasn't politically correct. What's politically correct, Pa?"

When I was a kid, the phrase hadn't existed, and as far as I was concerned it still shouldn't.

"Politically correct words and ideas are words and ideas that nobody minds talking about," I said. "Some people think Christmas isn't politically correct, so the schools don't want you to mention it even if you're thinking about it."

"It's not just me, Pa. All of my friends are thinking about it. Why isn't Christmas politically correct, anyway?"

I knelt down beside her. "Some people don't like it because they think it's too religious and other people don't like it because they think it's not religious enough and other people don't like it for other reasons. But in our family we like it. We don't think there are any ideas that are politically incorrect. You can talk about anything."

"How about the F-word, Pa? Is that politically correct?"

Hoist with my own petard. "It's just a word, Diana, but you're too young to be using some words and that's one of them. Later, when you're bigger, you can use it if you want to."

"What's it mean, Pa?"

Ye gods. "It can mean different things. Sometimes it's used when you're talking about love and sometimes when you're talking about hate. Sometimes it's part of a joke, and sometimes it's an insult. It's easy to use some words in a way you may not mean. That's why you should wait until you're older and know more about them before you use them."

"And the F-word is one of them?"

"That's right. My advice to you is not to use it for a while."

"Okay, Pa. But can I talk about Christmas?"

"Absolutely. Maybe not at school, but everywhere else."

"Good." She started for the library. Joshua, who had been listening to my language lore, started after her, but stopped when I called his name. He looked at me.

"Josh, I need some help on the computer. Maybe you can show me what to do."

"Sure, Pa." Joshua was used to my computer ignorance, and had total confidence in his own abilities.

"I want to get information about some people. I think the information is somewhere on the Internet, but I don't know

242

where or how to get it."

"I'll show you," said my son, and led me to the computer, which was already occupied by his sister.

She looked at us. There were two of us, and we were both bigger, but she was unintimidated. "It's my turn to be first," she said. "Yesterday I was second and we take turns."

"Aw, come on," said Joshua. "Pa has to do some work."

Her lower lip went out.

"No," I said. "If it's her turn, it's her turn. I can wait until you're both through."

I went out and left them with their homework, willing away my impatience. In the kitchen I made two perfect martinis and added black olives to Zee's and green ones stuffed with jalapeño peppers to mine.

"You're clouding," said Zee, reappearing and accepting her drink. She sat beside me on the couch in front of the fireplace.

I showed her the list of names, most of which I'd gotten from Kate, and told her what I knew about the people, and how I wanted to know more. Then I told her about the explosion.

"Good God!" she said. "It's a miracle Joe didn't get killed!"

"It wasn't a miracle; it was Joe's good judgment. He's been expecting something like that. In fact, if I hadn't phoned him and drawn him away from the house, he would have caught the Bunny in the act, so you could argue that it's my fault the Bunny is still walking around out there. That's why I need to know more about the people on this list. They were all in black ops or Kate's bed or both, and they're the only people I can think of who might be tied to this trouble on the island."

"Or might not be."

"If it's not one of them, fine. Whoever the guy is, he killed Arbuckle and he put a bomb in Toni's car. That means he's somebody Arbuckle trusted too much and that he either already knew or learned where Joe lived. Whoever he is, he's managed to hide out and move around the island at will in spite of the cops looking for him. I want to find out if anybody on that list knows the island well enough to do that, or was friendly with Arbuckle."

"The police and Jake Spitz and those DIA guys are following those leads," said Zee, the voice of sanity.

"Maybe I'll see something they miss."

She sipped her martini, then surprised me by saying, "Tell me about Kate."

I instantly decided not to tell her about my first meeting with Kate or about Kate's offer to share her bed and body.

"Kate is a very beautiful woman who likes men," I said.

"Does she like you?"

"She barely knows who I am."

"Have you had to fend her off?"

"She's a trained intelligence agent, so I probably couldn't fend her off if she really wanted to jump my bones."

"Would you try?"

"You bet." I hooked my arm around her and pulled her close.

"You're worried about her, though, aren't you?"

"The Bunny tried to kill her down in Bethesda," I said, "and she hasn't been seen since yesterday. So, yes, I'm worried about her."

"Did it occur to you that maybe she's the Bunny? That maybe she was lying about those awful needles in her apartment?"

"The idea crossed my mind, but I don't think so. She knows how to shoot and she's had Joe and me in the same room with her more than once. It would have been easy for her to kill us both and be back in Bethesda before anyone knew anything about it."

She shivered. "I hope the police catch the Bunny right away, before anyone else gets hurt."

Amen to that.

We were quiet for a while, sipping our drinks and looking into the timeless fire. Then Zee said, "You know who may be able to help you with the computer if Joshua can't manage it by himself?"

"Who?"

"Brady Coyne."

"Brady? I didn't know Brady was a computer whiz."

Brady Coyne lived in Boston and supported his fishing habit by lawyering for a wealthy clientele. We fished together when we could, and had an ongoing dispute about the relative virtues of fly casting, his game, and surf casting, mine.

"If he isn't, I'll bet he knows somebody who is," said Zee. "He must work with private detectives and they must subscribe to computer services that help them track down people. I've read that you can find out where people live, where they work, who they married, how many kids they have, and stuff like social security numbers and even bank accounts. I think it's scary, but I'll bet you that Brady knows somebody who can do that."

I gave her a kiss. "Have I told you lately that I love you?"

"Go stir your soup. I'll nip into the library and see how the kids are doing with their homework. After supper, we can attack your list."

So we did that. First Joshua gave the list a good shot. He got onto the Net and said, "Since you're looking for stuff about people, let's try typing 'people search.'"

He typed and clicked and up came a seemingly endless list of sites claiming to offer information about almost anybody. I patted Josh on the shoulder. Such a brilliant lad. Why hadn't I thought of doing that?

"Excellent," I said. "Let's see what we can find out about Samuel Arbuckle."

The site immediately wanted to know more about Sam: where he lived, his phone number, and especially his social security number.

"Try Alexandria as an address," I said.

He tried and there was Sam!

"Great. What can they tell us about him?"

What the site wanted before they told me more was money.

Hmmmmm. "Try another site," I said.

Joshua did that, and we found Sam

again, but again the site would only give up more information if I subscribed to its service.

I tried to calculate how much it would cost me to investigate all of the people on my list. Quite a lot. If the police would just let me in on what they could find out, I could save a bundle. But they wouldn't. There ain't no justice.

We tried three other sites with similar results. We'd been at it for an hour without any luck. Time for Plan B.

I thanked Joshua for his help and agreed with him that if I'd let him stay up and keep trying he might be able to find a site that would tell me everything I wanted to know for free. But I didn't want him staying up late on a school night, so I sent my disappointed boy to bed.

"Time to give Brady a call," I said to Zee.

Brady Coyne had recently moved to a place on Beacon Hill, where he cohabited with his lady, Evie. I had never seen his new house, but from my days on the Boston PD I knew it to be a place where not many cops could afford to live.

"Is this the same Brady Coyne who used to live a poverty-stricken life in an apartment looking out over Boston Harbor?" I asked when he answered on the first ring.

"How's fishing?" he asked in reply.

"Scalloping is about all we have to offer right now."

"If you can catch those with a fly rod, I may come down this weekend."

"You'll be happier if you wait for the bluefish to show up in May. The guest room is reserved in your name."

"I'll be there. What's happening down there in Eden?"

I told him what was happening and what I wanted. "Zee thinks you may know somebody who can get me the information," I said in conclusion.

He thought for only a moment and then said, "I think I might. I understand you've finally entered the twenty-first century and gotten yourself a computer, so I'll e-mail you the information in the morning. Now give me those names again. If you weren't so cheap you could do all this yourself, you know."

Good old Brady.

The next morning, after Zee and the kids had left for work and school, Brady's e-mail arrived. I printed it out. There was a surprising amount of information about the people on my list, but most of it meant little to me. I took my time going over it and had about decided that I'd wasted Brady's time when I noticed a small thing: Stephen Harkness, who'd gotten himself shot up on the trade mission, now worked for the FBI. I reread his file. He and his wife, Melanie, had three children and lived in Alexandria, Virginia. Melanie's maiden name was Oakland.

24

The little cogs began to turn in my brain and then bigger ones began to move. I thought back over things I'd seen and heard since Joe Begay had stepped into the shack where I'd been opening scallops. Then I reached for the phone and called Jake Spitz.

I got his assistant again. "You may remember me," I said. "We spoke a few days ago. I want to talk with Jake Spitz. Same subject as before: the Easter Bunny."

"One moment, please."

When Jake came on the line I said, "Can you get on somebody else's phone and call me back?" I gave him John Skye's number.

Jake said, "Yes," and hung up. Good old Jake. No questions asked.

Two minutes later John's phone rang.

"What's this all about?" asked Jake.

"Is your telephone assistant a guy named

Stephen Harkness? Used to work for the DIA?"

There was a short silence, then, "What about him?"

"I think he listens in on your telephone calls."

"Does he, now? What makes you think so?"

"Because whoever is trying to kill Kate MacLeod has known for days that she's here on the island, and the only person who might have figured that out from my phone call was you, because you know where I live. Unless your assistant listened to our talk last week. If he did, and knew my name, it wouldn't have been hard for him to learn I live on the Vineyard and to put two and two together. I figure he got interested when I mentioned the Easter Bunny."

"Why would he be interested in the Easter Bunny?"

"Because he knows it's not the Easter Bunny who wants to kill Kate MacLeod and Joe Begay. It's Steve himself."

Jake's voice was flat. "Why would Steve want to harm Kate and Joe?"

"How about revenge and jealousy? They've always been good motives for killing people. Harkness was Kate's lover, and even before he got hurt maybe he was jealous of her other lovers, including Edo and Joe Begay. Joe says he never slept with her and I believe him, but maybe Harkness thought he did. He was mad at Susan Bancroft, too, because she flipped him off when he tried to crawl into her bed."

"Go on."

"There's more. Harkness may think that somebody on his last mission — Kate or Edo or Susan or Joe Begay — stole his papers and got him crippled at the border crossing. Nobody knows what really happened to the papers, but it's easy to find new reasons to hate people you're already mad at."

"In case you didn't know," said Jake, with a hint of impatience in his voice, "Steve Harkness is in a wheelchair and will be for the rest of his life. He doesn't need legs to handle the phones, but he couldn't kill anyone if he wanted to. Besides, he's never missed a day of work here. You're barking up the wrong tree."

"I don't think he's the field agent," I said. "I think that's probably his brother-in-law, Stuart Oakland, who's up here right now, staying in his family's vacation house. Melanie, Harkness's wife, is Oakland's sister, and I think Oakland's motive is revenge for what the shock of Harkness's wounds did to her. When she learned what had happened to her husband, she apparently had a breakdown of some kind and had to be institutionalized. I think that Harkness blamed the mission crew and that Oakland believed Harkness."

I could hear Spitz breathing as he thought. Then he said, "I'll do some checking."

"Maybe you can check three things I'd like to know," I said. "Has Stuart Oakland had training that would make him proficient in the use of explosives and poisons? Did he know Sam Arbuckle? And what's become of Melanie Harkness?"

"I know what became of Melanie Harkness," said Spitz in a tired voice. "It's in our file on Steve. She got out of her room and up onto the roof of the sanatorium somehow and jumped before the nurses who were chasing her could stop her. The nurse who was closest to her heard her say, 'I'm flying.' But she wasn't flying."

I didn't know what to say to that, and so said nothing. But I could imagine my own feelings if I were in Stephen Harkness's or Stuart Oakland's place and believed what they believed.

Spitz's voice floated into my consciousness. "While I nose around here, I think you should offer your theory to the island police. If Oakland is the killer, he might decide to cancel his plans if they talk to him, even though they can't prove anything. Of course, they also might think you're full of baloney and ignore him."

"How can they ignore somebody who has that much motive and opportunity? Oakland has his own house and car. He knows the island and he was the first person to show up at Joe Begay's house after the explosion, maybe to check up on the results of his work. How can they ignore all that?"

"They don't know what you think you know. Besides, cops can ignore anything they want to ignore. If the police won't listen to you, try the DIA guys. Maybe you'll have better luck with them. They're probably looking for somebody to shoot."

"Call me if you learn anything."

"If I learn anything, I'll call Dom Agganis."

"Don't use your own phone," I said, annoyed. Nobody wanted to get close to me, to confide in me. Was it my breath? Had my deodorant failed?

Walking to my car, I noted that the temperatures had risen well above freezing and that the snow was melting fast. It felt more like April than December. New England weather; if you don't like it, wait a minute.

I drove to the state police office in Oak Bluffs and went inside. There I had the misfortune to find, not Dom Agganis or even some DIA men, but my nemesis Officer Olive Otero. Ours had been one of those instant mutual enmities that had begun the first time we met and had never changed. She was my Dr. Fell and I was hers.

"What do you want?" she asked.

"Your boss," I said.

"He's out. If you turn around and go out the door, you will be, too."

"I need to talk with him."

"If it's something relevant to the police, talk with me. Otherwise, go talk to the trees."

"I'll have to use some words with two or three syllables in them, and I don't want to confuse you. Where's Dom?"

"Out. You have something to say, say it. Otherwise, good-bye. I have work to do." She picked up a pen and slid a form under it. Since computers have become part of their office equipment, the cops have to fill out more forms than ever.

"I've never been impressed by your memory, Olive, so dig out your tape recorder and try to turn it on. I want Dom to hear what I actually say, not what you think I said."

"Gladly. I'll try to get some work done while you babble. When you're through, just leave. Don't bother saying good-bye."

She opened a desk drawer and brought out a tape recorder. "This is the microphone," she said, picking it up. "You talk into it. Got that?" She pushed a button and stated her name, the date and time, the address, and my name as the speaker. Then she put the mike in my hand and pretended to ignore me.

I told the tape recorder everything I'd told Jake Spitz and everything he'd told me. When I was done I put the mike on the desk. Olive turned off the recorder and waved at the door. "On your way, Jackson. We'll take it from here. Not that there's much to take."

"I hope for my country's sake that you're not the front line of national security," I said as I headed toward the door. There, just as I was about to go through, I whipped around in time to see her reaching for her phone. She glared and yanked her hand back, and I feigned a laugh and went on out, feeling foolish as I always did after one of my childish exchanges with Olive. I knew she must be good at her job or else Dom would have long since gotten rid of her, but I couldn't seem to prevent myself from deliberately rubbing her fur wrong. Perversity, thy name is Jackson.

I wondered if Olive would be able to reach Dom and, if so, what she would tell him. I was uneasy and felt time sliding past me. I drove toward the hospital, took a left on Eastville Road and a right on County Road. Buford Oakland's house was in one of the new developments off County. I turned in and drove to his house.

The Mercedes SUV wasn't in sight, but it could well be in the garage. I parked in the graveled circular driveway and knocked on the front door of the house. Nobody came to welcome me. I knocked again. Still nothing.

I noticed that the curtains on the living room windows had been pulled back to let in some winter light, and I peeked through one of them.

No lights were on.

I knocked again, just to be sure.

Nothing. Stuart Oakland was either out or wasn't receiving visitors.

I got out my key to the house and let myself in. I shut the door behind me and called out, announcing myself just in case somebody actually was home. Silence answered in the dusty way of empty houses.

I went through the kitchen and breezeway to the garage. The Mercedes wasn't there. I went back and walked through the house, not knowing what I expected to find.

All the rooms were empty. Stuart Oakland was sleeping in a second-floor guest room rather than in his parents' master bedroom. His bed was unmade and emitted a faint smell of sex. Was Stu making love to himself or to someone else?

I found two suitcases on a shelf of the closet and some clothes on hangers and in the drawers of a bureau. There was nothing unusual in the suitcases or among the clothes.

I went downstairs to the library. There were ashes in the fireplace. Apparently Stu sometimes spent an evening reading in front of a fire.

I took a look at his father's Civil War collection. Had Buford Oakland named his daughter Melanie after the character in *Gone with the Wind*? Had Melanie been raised as a delicate Southern belle? Was that why she'd become so unbalanced that she'd thought she could fly?

The LeMat pistol was in a slightly different position than before. I opened the glass cover of the table and sniffed the weapon, detecting a hint of detonated black powder.

As I sniffed again, I heard a muffled sound like tapping on a water pipe. I put the gun back on the table, closed the glass cover, and listened again. Sure enough, there was a tapping sound. Cold water pipes in the basement? I went to the stairs, flipped on the light, and walked down. At first everything seemed normal to me, then the sound came again. From a storage room on the far side of the basement.

I crossed over to the door and found it locked. The sound was from the other side. I went to Buford Oakland's workbench, found a pry bar, went back, and popped the padlock from the hasp.

Beyond the door, the room was black as a pit. I groped for a switch, found it, and flicked on the light. The room was full of dusty boxes, odd pieces of furniture, rusty tools, and other items not ever used but too good to throw away. Kate, naked, tied, and gagged, lay against the opposite wall, with her bound, bloody feet raised against a water pipe. She looked at me with gigantic eyes. As I stepped toward her I heard the sound of a door closing and footsteps on the floor above.

25

I was opening my pocketknife as I crossed the room.

Kate was bound tightly with what looked like clothesline, and was gagged with duct tape. I rolled her onto her belly and cut the ropes, glad that I hated dull knives and never carried one. Under my hands she was shivering from pain and the winter chill that had seeped into the basement. I saw that she was missing toe- and finger-nails.

I pulled the tape from her face as gently as I could, wrapped her in my coat, and whispered, "Can you walk?"

She gritted her teeth to keep them from chattering. "I don't know. I'm so cold."

I pulled her to her feet and she swayed against me. "We've got to get out of here," I said.

"Yes. I hear him. He's got a gun."

I, too, could hear the footsteps on the floor above. Kate took a step toward the door and then collapsed against me.

"I can't feel my feet," she said hoarsely "Leave me here and get away if you can."

I picked her up in my arms and went into the main room of the basement.

The footsteps moved toward the door leading to the basement stairs. There was no escape for us in that direction.

But I had been caring for this house for years and knew every inch of it. I crossed the room to the bulkhead door, let Kate's feet fall to the floor, and with one hand quietly opened both the door and the metal bulkhead above. Behind us, I heard footsteps carefully descending the basement stairs. Glad for the time I gained because Oakland was being wary, I swung Kate back into my arms and hurried up the stairs and out into the yard beside the house.

I didn't bother closing the bulkhead door but instead trotted around the house to the circular driveway where the Mercedes SUV was parked behind my old Land Cruiser. I opened the driver's door to my truck and literally threw Kate over into the passenger seat. Then I was behind the wheel, starting the truck and spinning gravel behind me.

The roar of my engine drowned all other sounds as a small hole appeared in my windshield. A glance in my rearview mirror showed a shattered rear window and Stuart Oakland taking aim for another shot. I ducked low and floored the gas pedal as another hole appeared beside the first and cracks like lightning bolts spread across the glass.

Then I was swerving out of the driveway and racing toward County Road, where a left turn would take me toward safety at either the state police station or the Oak Bluffs police station. But fate chose that moment to have a string of cars, headed by a slow-moving lady with gray hair and glasses, clog the far lane of the road, making a left turn impossible.

So I careened to the right and headed for the Vineyard Haven–Edgartown Road as fast as the old Land Cruiser would take me.

Beside me, Kate hugged herself and shivered, and I turned my heater as high as it would go, which wasn't much. I wished for the cell phone, but it was with Zee, so I concentrated on driving.

Our speed wasn't much, either, when compared with what Oakland's Mercedes could surely do, and it seemed certain that he would overtake us before I could reach either the Edgartown or Vineyard Haven police stations.

I squinted through my cracked windshield and kept flicking glances at my rearview mirror.

"Massage your wrists and ankles," I said to Kate. "Get the blood circulating again. Besides your nails, are you badly hurt?"

She began to rub the red rope burns on her wrists. Her voice was faint and filled with sorrow. "I'm hurt. I don't know how badly. I'm not as tough as I thought. I told him everything he wanted to know. Jesus."

"What did he want to know?"

"He wanted to know where to find Joe Begay."

"And you told him."

"Yes. I'd have told him anything. I'd have made up things. I'm a coward. I didn't know anyone could hurt as much as I did. I'd read about torture but I never knew what it's really like. I wanted to die but he wouldn't let me."

"Don't be hard on yourself," I said. "No one can stand up to torture." I was full of fear for Joe Begay. "Is that where he was when I found you? Out after Joe?"

"Yes. I think he only left me alive in case

I'd lied to him, so he could come back and get the truth. If he found Joe, he'd come back to kill me, too."

Topping a small hill behind me was what looked like the Mercedes. It was coming fast. I slowed but didn't stop at the intersection with the Vineyard Haven–Edgartown Road, then took a left, cutting off a pickup that was trying a left turn of its own onto County Road. The honking of the pickup's angry horn faded as I fled along the highway.

"Listen," I said. "I don't think we can outrun him all the way to Edgartown, so I'm going to go to my house. When we get there, we'll go inside as quick as we can. I've got guns there, and a phone. I don't know how he'll come at us, but I know he'll come."

Her small, shaky voice said, "Give me a gun. I can shoot without fingernails."

"Let's hope you won't have to."

As we passed the entrance to the Felix Neck Wildlife Sanctuary I could see the Mercedes closing on us. My old Land Cruiser was no match for it, but we still had a lead when I slammed on the brakes and swerved into my driveway. The Mercedes was already in view behind us when I skidded to a stop in front of the house, jumped out, yanked Kate over the driver's seat, and ran with her through the screened porch and on into the living room.

I kicked the door shut behind me, half threw Kate onto the couch, and ran to the gun cabinet. As I fumbled for the key, I heard the roar of the Mercedes as it came into the yard. Oliver Underfoot and Velcro came out of the guest room, yawned, and asked what was going on. I told them to go hide, but they ignored me.

I found the key, opened the cabinet, and snatched my father's twelve-gauge Remington. Its shells were in a box on the ammunition shelf. I dumped the box, slammed three shells into the magazine, and whirled toward the door, pumping a shell into the firing chamber as I turned.

Outside, I heard the sound of the Mercedes changing gears and moving. I peeked out the living room window and saw that Oakland had turned around and had parked in the driveway itself, blocking the only automobile exit. As I looked, he cut his ignition, opened the driver's side door, and slipped out of my sight beyond his car.

I shut the bolt lock on my front door, ran to the back door that led from the kitchen and closed that bolt as well, then trotted back to the living room, where Kate, wrapped in my coat, was gingerly limping toward the gun cabinet.

I pointed toward our bedroom and said, "I'll get you a gun; you go in there and get into some of Zee's clothes. Make sure you get boots and a coat. Keep an eye out the windows in case he circles the house."

She didn't argue. As I went to the cabinet she hobbled toward the bedroom. I ducked as Oakland fired a shot and one of our two living room windows shattered.

"The next thing that comes through will be a grenade," he shouted. "Just thought you'd like to know."

I yanked opened the cabinet, stuffed shotgun shells inside my shirt, grabbed Zee's competition Colt .45, found a loaded clip for the pistol, jammed it home, jacked a bullet into the firing chamber, flicked on the safety, and shoved the pistol in my belt.

Then, crouching, I ran to the front of the house, where I bobbed up and back down, snapping a look out the shattered window.

Nothing.

Where was Oakland?

I hurried to our other front window and peeked again.

Where was he, anyway?

Time to call the cops. I ran, bent, into the kitchen and picked up the phone. No dial tone. Oakland had cut the line. Even as this fact registered in my brain, the clock light on the microwave went out. He'd cut the power, too.

Kate limped out of the bedroom wearing Zee's clothes and winter boots under a quilted coat.

I handed her the pistol. "There's a full clip and one in the chamber. All you have to do is slip the safety."

She took the gun in her bloody hands and gave it the quick look of a person who's handled such a weapon before.

"He says he's got grenades," I said. "He's cut the phone and electricity. He's already set a bomb in one car, so he may really have grenades, too. He knows where we are, and we don't know where he is, so he's got that edge. Ours is that we can be in two places at once."

"My brain isn't working too well," she said, holding the pistol in one bloody hand and rubbing her forehead with the other. "I haven't eaten since yesterday. I need food."

I pointed at the refrigerator. "Help yourself, but keep a watch out the windows here while you're at it. If you see him, shoot him if you can. I'm going to circle through all the other rooms. Maybe I'll spot him from one of them."

But I didn't spot him until I was back in the living room again. There, through the broken windowpane, I saw him look quickly over the hood of the Land Cruiser then rear back as if to throw something. Without time to take real aim, I jerked the shotgun to my shoulder and fired. The shot spattered the hood of the truck but caused Oakland to spin away and throw wildly. Instead of hitting the house, his grenade arced into trees and detonated, sending branches flying.

There was a skittering of cat feet behind me as Oliver and Velcro scrambled for shelter under a bed. That would teach them to ignore my advice to hide. I pumped a new shell into the firing chamber and reloaded the magazine.

"No damage done here or there," called Oakland's voice from behind the Land Cruiser, "but I've got another grenade and this time it won't miss."

I suspected he was right.

"I'm not interested in you, Jackson," said the voice. "It's the woman I'm after. She's caused my family too much grief to live. Send her out and you get to keep your house and your life."

He was lying, of course, and I lied in return. "I've seen what you did to her. She can't even walk." I peeked over the sill and flicked my eyes this way and that, hoping to spot him long enough to get a shot.

"Carry her out, then, and save your own life. I won't shoot you, but I'll not wait long."

"Just hold your horses," I shouted, having no trouble putting fear in my voice.

I turned and ran back into the kitchen.

Kate was gone.

26

The back door was unbolted. I jerked it open and looked for Kate, but she wasn't to be seen.

Had she heard the exchange between Oakland and me? Did she really think that I'd turn her over to him?

I had no time to look for her. I went out the door, ran to the back corner of the house, paused, peeked around, saw no one, and ran to the front corner of the screened porch. There, I got down on my belly and snaked forward until I could take a fast look in the direction of the Land Cruiser, behind which I'd last seen Oakland.

I couldn't see him. I tried to look under the truck, hoping to catch a glimpse of his legs, at least, so I could shoot them, but the tall brown stems of last summer's flowers blocked my view. Damn! I knew I should have cleaned that flowerbed in the fall!

Was he still behind the truck? Or had he moved? Did he really have more grenades? I realized that somewhere deep inside me I was furious at the thought that he would blow up my house. I loved my house, and I especially didn't want it destroyed this close to Christmas! My children would be miserable!

Odd thoughts. I was being hunted by a killer and I was fretting about gardening and Christmas! Keep your mind on your work, J.W.

I threw a look behind me, in case Oakland had decided to abandon the Land Cruiser and circle the house. He wasn't there. Neither was Kate. Facing forward again, I wished I had more eyes, so I could look in every direction at once.

I took a deep breath, raised my head, and looked over the tops of the dead flowers.

Were those Oakland's legs, there on the far side of the front tire? Was he kneeling there because I'd winged him with that shot through the living room window? In his throwing arm, maybe? That would be nice. Even if he had more grenades, he couldn't throw them.

I pushed the shotgun carefully through the brown flower stems until I could get a sight on the legs. Were those really legs, or just shadows? If they were legs, I could damage him pretty severely, but if they weren't I'd give away my position, which was not a good spot for defense, being open on three sides.

Where was Kate? Running away through the woods, I hoped. Not that she could run. Limping away, then, keeping the shed between her and the house. Go, Kate! Find a house with a phone and call the cops!

I let out half a breath and fired at the legs. The shotgun kicked hard against my collarbone, but the legs didn't move. Damn! I jumped to my feet, put my back to the wall, jacked the old shell out and put a new one in, and ran, bending low, back toward the rear of the house.

I snapped a look around the corner and saw no one. Where the devil was Oakland? I looked at the shed. Did I see movement there? A shifting shadow? I flicked my eyes back and forth between the shed and the far back corner of the house, and shoved a new shell into the Remington's magazine.

All around the house, the pale, barren trees flowed away above the bronze-leafed ground until the earth and trees blended into an impenetrable wood. Was Oakland out there taking careful sight from behind some ancient oak or pine, like a modern Wind of Death? Lew Wetzel reborn?

Keeping low, I moved along the back of the house, passing the kitchen door, my head turning this way then that, fearing that moving shadow by the shed but at the same time suspecting it was more imagined than real, fearing, too, what lay around the corner I was approaching since Oakland, if he wasn't behind the Land Cruiser anymore, was certainly somewhere, perhaps just beyond that corner, waiting, knowing that sooner or later I'd come around it.

I reached the corner, threw a last look at the shed, saw nothing certain, and snapped a glance around the corner, pulling my head back almost before I put it out, hoping that if Oakland was there, his pistol wasn't pointing at the exact spot where my head appeared.

He wasn't there at all. Where was he? I could see the Mercedes in the driveway, but there was no Oakland. I swept my eyes in a half circle, looking into the trees that surrounded that portion of our yard.

Nothing.

Then several things happened very fast. Behind me, the kitchen door made a sound as it opened and Oakland stepped out. I turned, swinging the shotgun into line far too late, and saw Oakland aiming his pistol at me with a firm hand, and knew I was dead. But even as his finger tightened on the trigger, Kate was stepping out from behind my shed and crying, "Here I am!" She was aiming Zee's .45, held with a two-handed grip.

He was incredibly fast, spinning and firing at her even as she fired at him. His bullet rocked her and hers spun him around. She leaned forward and emptied the clip at him, staggering him as he fired back until, almost in slow motion, he lifted on his toes and pitched to the ground. At the same moment all her energy seemed to leave her and she, too, plunged to the earth.

My ears were full of noise. I had a feeling that wild activity was still going on although none was. I darted looks in every direction before I realized that nothing was moving or making sound.

I went to Oakland. His chest was moving slightly and blood was oozing out of him. His pistol was near a twitching hand. I kicked it away and went to Kate. She was lying on the brown leaves that covered the ground behind the shed. Her eyes were closed and her breath was shallow. I knelt beside her and opened Zee's coat and shirt. There was a bullet hole in her chest.

I ran back to Oakland and, ignoring the small noises he made, went through his pockets and found the keys to the Mercedes. I also found a DIA ID card with his picture on it. Why wasn't I surprised? I left it for the next guy to find then went back to Kate, picked her up, and carried her to the car, hoping I wasn't killing her.

I drove fast to the hospital and carried her into the emergency ward, shouting for help. Zee and other nurses came running and took her from me as I told them what had happened to her. A doctor appeared and she was rushed away on a gurney.

Zee was cool and professional. Before following the gurney she looked at me and said, "You've got blood on your coat. Are you all right?"

"Yes."

"Good. Stay and help fill out forms. I'll see you later."

She trotted out of sight.

I found a phone and called 911. I said who I was, reported a double shooting at my house and that one victim was still there but that I'd brought the other to the hospital, where I could be found at least for a while. I warned that no one should touch my Land Cruiser because it might be booby-trapped.

Then I called Joe Begay's cell phone. To my great relief he answered. He'd been in the woods and seen Oakland's Mercedes on Lighthouse Road, driving toward Uncle Bill Vanderbeck's house, but by the time he'd gotten to the house, Oakland was gone. I outlined what had happened before and after, and he said he'd drive down to Dom's office.

I was explaining to a hospital secretary just how little I knew about Kate's next of kin when Olive Otero arrived.

"You, of course," she said.

"Who else?"

"You don't look too good, but then you never do." She pulled a tape recorder from her pocket. "Why don't you give me the short version and we can get the long one later. Let's find a room where we can talk."

To my surprise she was attentive and patient. By the time I finished the short version, some Oak Bluffs cops, Sid Roebuck, and another DIA man were there, so I got to tell the whole story again. Dom, I learned, was with the Edgartown police and the other DIA men at my house, so I knew I had more storytelling ahead of me.

After a while, Zee walked into the room. I arched a questioning brow at her.

"Too early to tell," she said. "They've got her stabilized and they'll be taking her to Boston. Was the guy who tortured her the same one who shot her?"

"Yes."

"Is he still on the loose?"

"No."

"Good. Are you hurt at all?"

"No."

Then she let herself go a little bit. Tears came to her eyes and she came to me so we could hug each other. "Oh, you scare me sometimes! I wish you wouldn't!"

"It's all over," I said, holding her head against my chest and kissing her hair. "I love you. I'll tell you everything later."

"You'd better find yourself a lawyer," said Olive, when Zee had gone back to work. "The DA is running for reelection next year, and he may not believe those two shot each other, especially since the forty-five is yours. He'd love to have a spectacular win under his belt. Ex-cop behind bars, and like that."

"Thanks for waiting for my wife to leave before mentioning it."

"You're welcome," said Olive. "You know any good lawyers, emphasis on *good?*"

"A couple."

"If it happened the way you say it did, you should be okay, but if the woman doesn't make it or can't testify for some other reason, it'll be your word. The DA might get a lot of mileage out of that."

"It might not just be his word," said one of the Oak Bluffs cops. "Irma Quackenbush came into the station about forty-five minutes ago and wanted to arrest Mr. Jackson, here. Said he almost killed her at the junction of County and the Vineyard Haven–Edgartown Road. Said she knows his truck because he's one of those no-good hunters. Said she had to slam on her brakes so hard she stalled her pickup and that before she could get started again some other guy driving a hundred miles an hour almost hit her again. She was mad."

"Tell your lawyer about that," Olive advised me. She looked at the DIA men. "You two have anything to say or ask?"

The first shook his head, but Sid Roebuck was more talkative.

"The problem," he said, "is that Oakland and Arbuckle were both DIA, just like us. If Mr. Jackson, here, is telling the truth, Oakland was a rogue who may have killed three people."

"Did he and Arbuckle know one another?" I asked. "If they did, it would explain why Arbuckle let him get close."

"Arbuckle was a friendly guy," said Roebuck, "so it could have happened that way. A lot of people in the IC thought the Easter Bunny was the killer, so when Sam came up here to guard Kate he was expecting the Easter Bunny, not Oakland, and must have let his guard down. I probably would have done the same thing."

In the distance a siren was coming closer, and I thought it might be bringing Oakland to the hospital. Too late, I hoped.

27

Oakland was dead when the police got to my backyard, and for two days it was touch and go with Kate, but then things began to improve for her. After a week, it seemed clear that she would recover, and not much after that she was able to be interviewed by law enforcement officers.

Her testimony wasn't reported in the media, but from Zee's medical contacts with friends in Boston and from talking with Dom Agannis and the Chief in Edgartown, I learned that what she had told her inquisitors supported what I had told mine. The upshot of this was that our DA was now doing his best to take credit for stopping Oakland before he could kill again, rather than considering me for jail time.

By then I'd fixed the broken living room window and had the phone and electrical wires repaired. After the explosives experts had extracted a wired grenade from the Land Cruiser, thus showing that Oakland had had another one after all, I had replaced the truck's windshield and rear window. As soon as house and truck were back to normal, I moved my family home, where they belonged. The cats were glad to see us all and told us cat tales about how brave they'd been during Oakland's attack on the house.

On Friday, ten days before Christmas, it snowed. I'd been splitting wood until the first flakes began to fall, and had just finished stacking it when Joe Begay's truck came down the whitening driveway.

"I'm about to sit in front of a fire and have a little glass of something," I said. "Come in and join me."

"I will," he said, and sat while I put together mugs of tea improved with honey, lemon juice, cinnamon sticks, and rum. Delish.

"Toni and the kids home?" I asked, putting my feet on the coffee table, beside his.

He nodded. "Back from the rez. One of Toni's Christmas presents will be a new car."

"How's Kate doing?"

"Kate is doing better every day. We'll know she's back to normal when she gets a doctor in bed with her. I don't think it will be long."

"Quite a girl."

"She says she's getting out of the business. Going to settle down and raise a family."

"She mentioned getting married and giving up the wild life. Good luck to her husband, I say, whoever he may be."

We stared at the flames behind the glass-fronted stove.

"I thought you might be interested in the news and guesswork out of Washington," said Begay. "Jake Spitz called this morning and gave me the latest facts and speculation."

I said nothing, and he went on: "Stephen Harkness has been persuaded to talk. I didn't ask how, and your guesses turn out to have been pretty good. When Melanie Harkness jumped, both he and her brother blamed the whole mission crew. Oakland got friendly with Susan, drugged her, and then shot her full of enough dope to kill a horse. Then he tried for Kate in Bethesda, but missed her. It wasn't hard for him to learn that I live on the Vineyard, so he came here to find me." He gave me a humorless smile. "He even had you get his house ready for him."

"Good grief," I said, "that means I was almost an accessory before the fact to my own murder. We live in complicated days."

Begay sipped his tea, licked his lips, and made a contented sound. "Good stuff. You helped him again when you phoned Spitz. Harkness listened in and did some thinking and then called Oakland and told him that Kate must be here, too."

"Two for the price of one," I said.

"It was just a matter of finding us, and it helped him out when some people in the DIA and other IC people, including some in my outfit, got it into their heads that the Easter Bunny was the hunter. That idea took attention away from other candidates long enough for Arbuckle to be sent up here to find Kate and watch her back.

"But it wasn't the Bunny who was after her, it was Oakland, and the current theory is that Oakland played hail-fellow-well-met with Arbuckle and arranged to meet him off on some empty side road to confer."

"And when Arbuckle showed up, Oakland shotgunned him, but Arbuckle got away as far as my place."

"The shotgun is a problem," said Begay,

"because Oakland's piece was a Beretta nine millimeter."

"I imagine that he didn't want to use his own gun to kill Arbuckle," I said. "Besides, a shotgun wound was a lot better because it might make people think Arbuckle was a hunting accident."

"Makes sense to me," said Begay, nodding, "but they haven't found the shotgun, and if Arbuckle had seen one, he should have been less trusting."

I'd been thinking about that. "Try looking in the glass-covered case in Oakland's library," I said. "Have the shotgun barrel of that LeMat revolver tested. I'll bet it's been fired recently. Oakland couldn't hide a shotgun, but he could hide the LeMat in plain sight."

Joe nodded. "I'll drop that idea into Dom Agganis's ear. He'd like to get as many loose ends as possible tied into a nice knot."

Cops almost never got all the loose ends of a case tied into a nice knot, but they always tried.

As Oakland was pulling off Kate's nails, he'd enjoyed telling her how he'd found her, and I thought about how fate so often takes a hand in the games men play.

Her habits were pretty well known. She

liked men and she liked bookstores. This time of year the bookstores were closed at night, but the bars were open, so he spent his evenings parked on the streets watching bar traffic. And fate had decreed that he was looking in the right direction when she went into the Fireside. It wasn't just luck, but there was a lot of luck in it. If she'd gone to Edgartown that night, everything would have been different.

By the next morning he'd burned her clothes in the library fireplace and she'd told him everything she knew, including where to find Joe's house. Then he'd gone to Joe's house and wired the car he found there, but fate had again taken a hand and his effort had failed. By the time he came home and saw my truck in his driveway, the Norns had rewritten his script.

"Listen," I said, "why don't you and Toni and the kids come for lunch tomorrow? Afterward, we're going out in the woods to cut our Christmas tree. The ladies and the kids can run around in the snow while I chop and you give advice."

"Sounds good," said Joe. He looked into the bottom of his mug. "You got any more of this stuff?"

I did, and he and I were still sampling it

in front of the fire when Zee and the kids got home.

The next day, after a warm lunch, we all went out into the still-falling snow, I with my coil of rope and my sharp ax over a shoulder. The flakes were big and soft and light, and there was no wind. Silent snow, secret snow. It clung to the branches of the trees and turned the world into a white wonderland.

We scuffed our way out through the woods behind the house, kicking clouds of snow as we went, making snowballs and throwing them, planning a snowman for the front yard. In time, one child, then another, then all four of them flopped down and made snow angels with swinging arms and legs. Toni and Zee, inspired, joined them, and finally Joe and I did, too. When we rose there was a family of snow angels beside our path.

A quarter of a mile from the house, we came to the clearing I was looking for. On its far side was the perfect fir tree I'd been watching grow for the last three years.

In the clearing I had the children follow me in making a large circle, then forming four straight spokes to the center of what was now a proper wagon wheel on which to play fox and the geese. Joshua elected to be the fox and the other children and their mothers were the geese. On my signal, the game was on, with the fox pursuing the geese around the rim and in and out of the spokes of the wheel in the latest edition of that ancient game of tag.

While Zee and Toni and their children ran and slipped, and laughed and screamed, Joe and I went to the fir tree, shook the snow off it, and stomped the surrounding snow flat. On my knees I swung the sharp ax and felled the tree, feeling a familiar mix of guilt for killing it and happiness at the thought of the magical, ornamented wonder it would soon become: our Christmas tree. The tree of life renewed.

I tied our rope around its trunk and when the fox and the geese were all red-cheeked, exhausted, and happy, Joe and I teamed up and, half pulling, half carrying the tree, led our families back to the house through the endless, falling snow.

The next day Zee and I and the kids decorated the tree. My job, as always, was to put the star at the top and then to string the small white lights. After that came the hanging of balls and other ornaments. This was done according to the height of the hanger. I hung the small ones that went nearest the star, Zee hung the middle branches, and Joshua and Diana handled the low ones. When we were done, it was the finest tree we'd ever seen, and Oliver Underfoot and Velcro crawled under it, purring, as if it were their very own.

That night as I was tucking Diana into bed, she looked up at me with sleepy eyes and said, "Pa, I'm glad we're back in our house, and I love Christmas more than almost anything, don't you?"

"More than anything but you and Joshua and your mother and Oliver and Velcro," I said.

"Are we going to sing carols this year?"

"Absolutely. I'll play my guitar and we'll all sing. You can't have Christmas without carols."

"Pa?"

"Yes."

"I love you."

"And I love you. Now go to sleep. Tomorrow is a school day."

I went out and sat beside Zee in front of the glass-doored stove. I put my arm around her shoulders and felt good and wondered if, in spite of the Oaklands and Harknesses of the world, Longfellow had been right about the Christmas bells: that when they pealed loud and deep, they sang that wrong shall fail and right prevail, with peace on earth, goodwill to men.

Christmas was the right time for such hope, and I let myself feel it as I looked into the fire.

RECIPES

Scallops Tikka

1 lb. bay scallops
Mix together about 4 tbsp. each of:
Tikka paste (available in Indian ethnic food section)
Sour cream or plain yogurt (amounts may be varied to your liking)
Crackers or buttered bread crumbs
Cajun seafood seasoning

Gently stir scallops into mixture. Remove scallops and spread in single layer in greased ovenproof pan. Sprinkle with buttered bread or cracker crumbs seasoned with a small amount of Cajun seafood seasoning.

Preheat the broiler. Broil 3 to 4 inches from heat for about 5 minutes.

Serves 4

Scallops in Sherry-Mustard Sauce

1 lb. bay scallops
4 tbsp. fresh thyme, chopped
Juice of 1 lemon
1 tsp. extra-virgin olive oil
2 tbsp. dry sherry
1 tbsp. Dijon-style mustard
Chopped Italian parsley

Mix scallops with thyme and lemon juice. Heat oil in skillet and sauté scallops for about 1 minute. Remove scallops to warm plate. Add sherry, mustard, and reserved marinade to skillet. Bring to a boil. Reduce slightly and pour over scallops. Sprinkle with chopped parsley.

Scallops may be served over rice or linguini.

Serves 6

Scallops in Wine

2 lbs. scallops
1 ¼ c. dry white wine
¾ tsp. salt
⅛ tsp. pepper
1 bay leaf
1 celery stalk (with leaves)

¼ tsp. dried thyme leaves
2 tbsp. chopped pimiento
¾ c. water
½ c. butter
½ lb. fresh mushrooms, sliced
¼ c. chopped green onion
¼ c. chopped green bell pepper
¼ c. flour
2 egg yolks
¼ c. heavy cream
¼ c. buttered bread crumbs
¼ c. grated Parmesan cheese

In medium saucepan, combine scallops, wine, salt, pepper, bay leaf, celery, thyme, pimiento, and water. Bring to boil, reduce heat, and simmer, covered, for about 5 minutes. Drain scallops, reserving liquid. Discard bay leaf and celery.

In 4 tablespoons butter, sauté mushrooms 2 minutes. Add onion and green pepper and sauté 5 minutes more. Set aside.

Melt the rest of the butter, remove from heat, and stir in flour until smooth.

Gradually stir in reserved liquid from scallops. Bring to a boil, stirring constantly, reduce heat, and simmer 1 minute.

In small bowl, mix egg yolks lightly with cream. Stir in some of hot mixture, then add egg mixture to sauce. Cook, stirring, over low heat, about 5 minutes or until thickened.

Combine all ingredients except the bread crumbs and grated cheese; pour into individual baking shells or into baking dish. Top with buttered crumbs and Parmesan cheese. Bake in a preheated 400-degree oven for 15 minutes or until brown and bubbly.

Serves 8

About the Author

Philip R. Craig grew up on a small cattle ranch southeast of Durango, Colorado. He earned his MFA at the University of Iowa Writers' Workshop and was for many years a professor of literature at Wheelock College in Boston. He and his wife live on Martha's Vineyard.